THE LAST HOMESTEAD

MARIE WILKENS

1

The Beauford County Herald
On June 16th, the country will experience what is forecasted to be the first major solar shower event in the planet's history. However, only a few pinpointed locations will be affected by this phenomenon. Of the three half-mile radii "hit points," there is only one expected in the United States. The other two, in Egypt and the Netherlands, are expected to hit fields and deserts. Stateside, the government has secured a ten-mile "buffer zone" around the potential area located just a mile off the California coast.

Between the hours of one and four on Saturday morning, you'll be able to see the event in the night sky. We'd like to remind our readers that the national government has issued a statement reiterating that this event is going to be a small one, and they are well prepared for any surprises. We are sure this will be an exciting event to witness, but we caution our readers *to have a readiness bag prepared for any natural disaster, no matter how severe or localized.*

2

Sarah Fowler plucked the onion off her sandwich and cursed under her breath. She hated raw onions, a detail the man behind the counter at the sub shop earlier in the afternoon was made aware of. The disgruntled teen had taken one look at her corrections officer uniform and quickly made his own assumptions. She didn't care that he smelled like pot. Sarah had been a teen once. In the lit teen's haste to get her and her sidearm out of the store, he must have heard the word *onion* and presumed she'd wanted them.

"So, they approved your vacation time? I'd hate to think of you missing work on our behalf," Connie Fowler said.

Sarah rolled her eyes. "Mom, I've been taking the same six weeks off every fall for the past five years. They aren't going to change their minds for year six, okay? It was approved by the captain months ago."

"Well, as long as you aren't going to get into any trouble over it," Connie said.

As much as she adored the near-daily calls from her parents, Sarah was anxious to get off the phone. It was always the same conversation whenever they talked about her vacation time. Every year Sarah would make the trip from Florida to her parents' ten-acre homestead on the Maine coast. For six weeks in the fall, she would spend her days harvesting the summer crop and helping manage the small roadside stand they ran annually for incoming tourists arriving to watch the changing of the leaves. It was something Sarah looked forward to every year.

When she'd first started at Glenwood Central Correctional Facility, the six weeks of leave were conditional to her employment there. Not once in her time at the facility had she called off or taken a sick day beyond the vacation she had planned yearly. Sarah was obsessive about staying healthy just so she could make it home to her parents every autumn. At seventy-five and eighty-one, Sarah's late arrival in their lives had been a surprise but a blessing if you asked Connie and Henry.

"How are the crops looking this year?" Sarah asked. "The cold weather has to be taking a toll."

"Actually, despite how cold it's gotten this year, the orchard is thriving. We're close to having one of the best seasons we've had in years."

"That's great. I half expected you to tell me that half the crop was lost. I'm glad to hear that's not the case."

Connie chuckled. "Not this year."

"If the orchard is still doing so well, how about the greenhouse? Is it doing just as good as you expected it would?"

"Oh, it's really booming. We expect it to keep up with the orchard. Overall, everything is going very well this year. Your dad couldn't be happier."

"I figured he'd have a good year. He always does when the crops do well. I'm sure that between the two of them, you're staying fairly busy."

"Well, considering we're not getting any younger, I think we're doing pretty good," Connie said. "It keeps us busy, and there are some days we can barely keep up, but you know how your father is. Nothing can keep that man down."

"Daddy's always been the busy type. I can't wait to get up there and see you guys this year."

"Is everything going okay at work?"

"Of course. I just look forward to seeing you every year. I'm hoping to get out on the boat with Henry this year."

"Speaking of the boat, Henry thinks the lobster harvest is going to be great. He's more optimistic than I have ever seen."

"Do you think Dad will wait to take out the boat until I get up there?" Sarah asked. "I'd like to give him a hand if he can hold on that long."

"Well, like I said, you know how he can be. I honestly don't know if he's going to wait for you or not."

Sarah chuckled and shook her head as she tossed the remnants of her lunch into the trash bin next to her desk. Henry Fowler was a stubborn old man. He'd long ago retired from his fishing boat but still took it out in the fall for the local harvest when only seasonal fishermen could catch the acclaimed Maine lobster. The money the homestead brought in during the four weeks the roadside stand was open would see it through the rest of the year. The elderly couple was beloved by everyone, locals and returning tourists alike. Sarah wouldn't miss it for the world.

Captain Harden, in earnest, hadn't been thrilled. For the first time since she'd been hired, the six weeks of leave fell during the same time as their five-year state review. The facility would be crawling with state officials, reporters, and extra personnel. It was no surprise, given how well it was run. As a level-one facility, it had one of the best rehabilitation rates in the state. That was accredited to Harden's rule, which she, in turn, shared with the staff. It was a well-oiled machine and a pleasant work environment. But no career would ever be higher on Sarah's list of priorities than her parents. Family came first.

Her mother was still rambling about the greenhouse, something about the tomatoes coming in early, but Sarah's mind had drifted away. She quickly pulled her attention back to the conversation as the alarm on her phone alerted her that her break was nearly up.

"Okay, Mom. I have a ton of things to take care of before I can make this trip and take my vacation. I'll have to call you later," Sarah said.

"Well, I'll let you go then. When you head out this way, make sure you do it safely," Connie said. "Are you prepared for this little solar storm they've been talking about on the news? It's been the talk of the town for the last few weeks."

Sarah chuckled. "I'm sure we're going to be fine. The reports here have it listed as a normal thing that happens every so many years."

"I meant at work, honey. Do they have proper precautions set up at your facility? They're saying there will be some power outages."

"We have plenty of precautions for power outages. The generator is top of the line, and we have a certain protocol for everything else. We're going to be fine here."

"I hope so. If not, you know our safety plan, right?"

"Mom, I don't think we should have to worry about that. In this day and age, it would take an act of war to shut us down. I'm not all that concerned about it, if I'm being honest."

"Either way, you know the plan. We have everything we need to get through just about anything, but you can never be too prepared."

Sarah groaned. "It's 2023. We aren't going to need a failsafe plan. Nothing is going to happen, and if it does, it won't take everything out like that."

"I just want you to be careful. We'll see you soon."

"All right, Mom. I love you, guys. Don't worry; we're well protected down here."

As she ended the call and her timer started to chime, Sarah clocked back in on her computer. Before heading out to do her walk-through, she scanned the monitors that covered the west wall of her office. From her position, Sarah could see everything that happened not only in her cell block but the others as well. Sarah was the officer in charge of the night shift. Any problems in her block or the other three would go directly to her. The pay bump and accreditation on her record were worth the added responsibility.

Then again, she had never shied away from moving up in her career. From an early age, Sarah knew she wanted to be in corrections. While her parents had always advocated for her to join law enforcement, Sarah had known most of her life about the gray areas involved in the career path. She simply couldn't bring herself to put the law above the lives of her fellow mankind. In more than one instance, a prisoner had come to them not because they were guilty but because they'd crossed the wrong politician, political figure, or officer.

Stretching out as she stood, Sarah knocked the rest of her lunch garbage into the trash and tucked her phone into the pocket of her cargo pants. It would stay on vibrate for the rest of her shift, but she could still feel it if there were an emergency and her parents needed to reach her. As she headed out into the main cell block, Sarah looked around in the dim silence and smiled. In two months, she would be back home in Maine with six weeks to rest, relax, and enjoy the life she'd created as a child. Until then, there was work to be done.

3

As she moved through the empty halls in a pattern Sarah knew by heart, she thought about her work and the checklist running through her mind. It was the same every night except for Thursdays, the one day she took off each week. Now, with it being halfway through her Friday shift, Sarah found herself looking forward to the walk-through. It was always interesting to see what had changed during her day off. Staying on top of all the changes was part of her job as the officer in charge.

Everything was quiet and peaceful, just the way she liked it. Making her way to the large break room where the inmates spent their afternoons and time off from their jobs in the facility, she noticed a familiar figure approaching, and she waved. Alan Elliot was her second in command and the only other officer she would see until the end of her shift if there weren't any problems. Sarah could keep watch over the other guards at their own cell blocks thanks to the cameras in her office. That didn't stop her from making rounds every once in a while to the other buildings when it was a nice night outside.

With the potential for a power outage, even the incredibly slim chance they had, Sarah would stay put in her own cell block unless needed. She wanted to be able to deal with any emergencies that might arise. Sarah wasn't anticipating any power outages from the solar event, but it never hurt to be prepared. The correctional facility's power outage plan placement was clear. The OIC needed to be in a location where the others could find them at a moment's notice. Closing the distance between Alan and herself, Sarah grinned and shook her head when she saw the Tupperware container in his hands.

"Spaghetti and meatballs is the meal of the night," Alan said, handing her the container.

"You know that wife of yours is going to make me fat," Sarah replied.

"I can't stop her from cooking meals for you. Becky just wants to make sure you're eating good meals and staying healthy. Plus, she loves to cook."

Becky had been sending Alan to work with meals for her for as long as she could remember. Being single and working long hours meant a lot of fast food and prison meals. If she felt bad about anything the prisoners were subjected to, it was the food. She'd eaten some prison food in the many years she had put in at the correctional facility, and Sarah was less than impressed. She was thankful Alan's wife had a soft spot for her.

Sarah smiled. "She's definitely got a knack for it. You'll have to tell her thank you for me."

"I'll let her know, just like I always do. You're going to have to make it over for some quality time soon. Becky would like to see you."

"I'll make some time to do that when I get back from vacation," Sarah said. "What's the block feeling like today?"

"It's been a quiet day," Alan replied. "There hasn't been any drama. At least nothing that we've been able to catch."

"These are the days we hope for. I would appreciate a nice, easy day."

"Well, so far, so good. I'm going to head out for lunch. Do you need anything from me before I go?"

"Nope. I should be good to go. You go ahead and take your lunch break. I'm just going to finish my rounds before heading back to the desk."

"All right. I'll be back in a bit."

Despite knowing she wasn't supposed to play favorites with any of her subordinates, Alan was the exception she made to the rule. He'd been the man responsible for getting her in the door at the facility. Alan had no desire to move up the ladder at the facility.

His position there provided him and his family of five with insurance and benefits. Becky's work as a doctor at the local hospital gave them everything else they needed. He loved working with the inmates and helping rehabilitate them. It was the only aspect of her elevated position that Sarah didn't love.

It was easier to help the inmates when you had a good relationship with them. Sarah's evenings were, more often than not, spent checking spreadsheets and reviews from the shift before when she wasn't making schedules and checking for intake and release updates. It was all work that needed to be done, but it kept her off the floor more than she liked. There were still a handful of cases and inmates she kept an eye on. It broke her heart when a new arrival would come through that had obviously been railroaded by the system.

Those cases kept her up at night. She would pour over the files for hours as soon as she walked through the door. Most times, it would be while she scarfed down the cold leftovers Becky sent with Alan. There were men who deserved to be there, men who admitted what they had done, and those bad seeds who were only at the low-level facility because of deals they'd struck. More often than the general public realized, there were those who had no right to be imprisoned whatsoever. Those few gave her purpose and a reason to keep climbing the ladder. Even if it meant changing the system one convict at a time, at least she was doing something.

As she made her final round through the cells, her

mind floated back to the conversation with her mother earlier in the day. It wasn't often she took anything the news reports had said to heart, but the solar storm happened to be one of them she had kept an eye on. According to the report, her area wasn't supposed to be affected by it. The pass was supposed to take place farther north. She chuckled at the thought of her parents prepping for a storm that would, at its worst, cause a few power outages. Suddenly, she heard an inmate calling her name.

"What are you doing, John?" Sarah asked, turning to the man's cell door.

"Just want a few minutes to chat. My cellmate has been down in the infirmary all day, and I've had no one to talk to," John said.

"That's fair, but you have to be excited that your time is almost up. Are you going to keep your nose clean this time around?"

"I'm thinking about it. I know one thing for sure."

"Yeah? What's that?"

"I ain't going to be robbing any banks. I don't think I can go through another round of prison."

"I think you're moving in the right direction. This place has made an impression on you, and I'm glad to know you're going to get out there and do the right thing."

"I owe a lot of that to you. Say, have you been watching the news and what they're saying about this solar flare?" John asked.

"Yeah, but it's supposed to go through up north. We're going to be just fine down here."

John chuckled. "I sure was hoping it would do something around here. It certainly would break up the monotony around this place. Anyway, you have yourself a good night."

"You too, John."

There was one more stop she wanted to make before returning to her office and spending the bulk of the remaining six hours on her shift doing paperwork. Inmate 6735 was seven doors from the steps that led to her office in what they affectionately called the crow's nest. She had a 360-degree view of her block. Her heart lurched a little at the thought of the inmate leaving. It wasn't a romantic affection but a deep one, nonetheless. How many more days would she have where he would be her last stop before payroll forms, intake papers, and quarterly reports?

Like a handful of others, he was not a guilty man, and she didn't need the paperwork to tell her so. Her gut instinct was never off when it came to people. She knew the guilt of every inmate at the facility. Sarah swallowed and shook her head, reminding herself that it was all part of the job.

Drawing a ragged breath, she absentmindedly fidgeted with her uniform to make sure it was free from crumbs and wrinkles before moving past the steps leading to her office to the other side of the block. She and Adam had been working John's case together despite the backlash she'd gotten from Captain Harden. In the end, Sarah knew Harden liked to see the innocent people Sarah helped go free. She was a good woman despite her tough exterior.

4

Adam Smith was coming up on his tenth anniversary at Glenwood. While she hadn't been there for the first half of his stint, she'd met him her first day at the facility and known him even longer than that, thanks to the media circus that had surrounded his trial. The case had captured the nation's attention for weeks that summer. She had been sixteen, and Adam Smith had been a heartthrob at eighteen years old. While the prosecutors had painted Adam as a murderous, scorned lover who heartlessly slaughtered his pregnant ex-girlfriend, Adam had pleaded innocence.

He claimed their relationship had ended on good terms, with a co-parenting plan in place for the birth of their child when she'd started a job at the county sheriff's office as a receptionist. Adam's claim that one of the younger officers quickly became obsessed with her fell on deaf ears. The jury had returned with a verdict within an hour of being released. Adam Smith was found guilty and sentenced to life in prison without the possibility of parole. His pleas of corruption within the police station fell on deaf ears for eight years until tragedy struck the small outlying Florida town Adam was from.

Two of the officers who had testified against Adam were found to have done some terrible things throughout their careers. Lying under oath to get a wrongful conviction was the least of what they'd done. Unlike the movies, Adam wasn't suddenly free and walking the streets because it was discovered that a few cops had lied. There was a process to appeal a case and everything needed to be redone. While Sarah was hopeful that his conviction would soon be overturned, Adam didn't hold out the same hope, though she could understand why. Being institutionalized was a truly terrifying process.

Sarah tapped on the bars of Adam's cell. She could tell the man had been waiting for her to arrive. It had become quite the routine when she would stop by his cell daily. The system had failed him, and not only was it something known within the facility, but the national news had made it the center of daily conversation and updates. Adam smiled at her and approached the cell door.

"You're late today."

"A few minutes is nothing in a day in the life of a prisoner. Besides, did you have some big plans that I've made you late for?"

Adam chuckled. "You don't know, I could have had something important I needed to do."

"Well, in that case, I apologize," Sarah said. "I'll try to make sure I do better from now on. At least until they let you out of this place."

"Hell, if they were going to release me, they would have done it by now. I'll believe it when I see it at this point."

"They're going to make the right decision, Adam. You don't belong here, and I'm sure they're going to make a decision soon. We might even hear something by Monday. I think we're going to get some good news."

"I'm not going to hold my breath on that. Those people have left me here to rot, and I'm sure they don't want the world to know how badly they screwed up."

Sarah sighed. "You have to keep hope alive, Adam. Don't let their failures control how you think about things. You're going to get out of here, and I, for one, think it's going to be soon. Have you started making plans for when you get to leave?"

"I'll think more about that once I cross those lines out of the front gate. Until then, I'm going to keep my mindset right where it is. I can't afford to think outside of those gates until they let me go."

Sarah cringed and shook her head. She could understand his hesitation toward having hope, but she wasn't going to stop being upbeat because of it. They were polar opposites but somehow managed to click. Yet she didn't dare have hope that they could be friends once he headed out. She could be optimistic for him but knew once he was free, he'd find his own path and forget all about her after years of having her ruling over him. Refusing to let her sadness show, she smiled at her friend again.

"You heard about this storm coming?" Sarah asked, not yet ready to leave.

He grinned and nodded. "Sure have. You've gotta love how much the media blows things out of proportion."

Sarah agreed with him, and Adam knew it. They had spent hours talking about their upbringings. It was amazing to hear how similar they had been despite being worlds apart. His father had taught him how to live off the land just like her parents. The only difference between them was the income level of the people raising them. Sarah had been given every opportunity in life, whereas Adam had fought for everything he'd gained by the time he was tossed in jail. She watched him as he leaned against the bars, his eyes looking out the small windows high above the first-floor cells.

Dark tendrils of hair fell into his eyes. Sarah was sure the hair he kept long shielded his inquisitive gaze from the other inmates. They didn't like it when people watched them, no matter who it was. She prided herself on the prison having an incredibly low rate of violence and inmate fighting. If there were problems between the inmates, they worked together to solve them before the warden needed to be involved.

"You're looking a little like you're lost in thought," Adam said. "Everything going okay for you?"

"Yeah. I'm just thinking about when they let you out. How different things are going to be, but you're finally going to get to see the real world and how much it has changed."

"I'm sure it's going to be crazy at first, but I haven't given it much thought. Say, you going to throw me a big party when I get out?"

Sarah laughs. "I'd throw you the biggest party you've ever had if I thought for one moment that you'd actually show up."

"Well, I could tell you I would come to that, but after what I've seen with the corruption in this country, I'm getting out as soon as I can."

"Planning on getting yourself out of the country then?"

"Yes, ma'am. As soon as I leave these gates, I'm getting as far from this country as I can," Adam said.

"Have you given any thought as to where you're going to go?"

"Actually, I have some family down in Argentina. That will be the best place for me, and I'll be back with my relatives. I think out of everybody, they deserve to have me back home."

"That's good, Adam. I think it will be great for you to get some quality time with your family. Especially with how long it has been since you've seen them. Well, I need to get some work done before they fire me. I'll catch up with you later."

"They'd be making a big mistake if they ever fired

you."

It irritated her to no end that she was so bothered by Adam's revelation. Of course, he would have family and people who cared about him somewhere in the world. It was a good thing he wasn't going to be alone. Yet the twinge inside her remained as she climbed the metal steps to her crow's nest. Unlocking the door, Sarah plopped down in her chair and swiveled around to look out over the block. It was going to be a long weekend with everyone on edge over the threat of the solar storm. There was no point in telling the inmates not to get worked up over it.

They had something to do and something to focus on. As long as it wasn't causing them any problems, she didn't see the harm in letting them hope for an outage. The old buildings would quickly become hotboxes, and they'd regret wishing the power would shut off, even for the five minutes it would take for the backup generators to kick in. They were protected by overlaying fencing woven with gold thread in an effort to protect against the threat of a solar flare. She had done enough research on the topic to know if a major solar storm struck them, the protective cages wouldn't do much good for the generators.

Shaking her head, she did her best to let it slip from her mind. The threat was minimal, and the prisoners would stay locked behind the doors no matter what surges might come. It was in her nature to worry about every little thing that might go wrong. The reality was that nothing was going to happen, and she knew it. They were protected not only as a facility but as a nation. She had faith in their predictions and needed to get back to work.

5

Sarah combed over the payroll for the last two weeks. It wasn't due to be turned in until the following Wednesday, but she liked to have everything ready in case of an emergency. Her parents weren't in their fifties anymore. If she needed to rush to Maine for any reason, everything would be done for whoever had to step in and help out while she was gone. While no catastrophes had hit yet, there was nothing wrong with being prepared. Tucking the file back into its place in her desk, she locked the drawer and tapped on her keyboard.

The computer screen jumped to life in front of her, blinding her for a split second. Immediately, she clicked on the internet icon. She and the other COs were the only ones who could access the outside world from their work computers. She took the privilege to heart and only checked her personal email once every shift most of the time. Tonight was different, though. She had kept something back from Adam.

Earlier in the day, a friend of hers at the prosecutor's office had updated Sarah on Adam's case. As of three that afternoon, it was sitting in front of a judge, waiting to be dismissed. When she'd told him there was a chance he'd be a free man come Monday morning, she hadn't been exaggerating in the least. It was the reason she was now checking her email. If Larry Barns, an attorney with the prosecutor, had learned anything, he promised to email her no matter how late it was.

Slowly the computer connected to the internet and loaded the page after working its way through the plethora of firewalls. Twenty seconds later, her email was loaded, and she was scanning through a dozen junk emails when the computer pinged, and a new email came through. Her heart started to race as she dug out her phone and dialed Larry's number.

"Hey, Sarah," Larry said. "Did you get a chance to read the email I sent to you?"

"I certainly did. Is everything in there?"

"It's all there, Sarah. The judge signed off on the whole thing at about midnight. He made a notary meet him at the courthouse just to make sure everything was taken care of."

"I can't believe it's finally going to happen. He's been waiting a long time for this."

"I know he has, and I'm glad I get to be the one who delivers the news to you," Larry said. "I wanted to get the paperwork over to you as soon as I got word. As of right now, only a handful of people know about it."

"So, there's nothing else keeping this from happening?"

"Nope. The judge made sure to do everything by the book. There was no way he was keeping Adam in there for more time when he's been proven innocent."

Sarah sighed in relief. While Adam had his reservations about getting released, she knew they were going to do the right thing. There was a lot of corruption within the system, but the world had grown up with all its new technology. Word had spread quickly about his wrongful conviction, and the growing number of people asking for his release couldn't be ignored. Come Monday morning, Adam was finally going to be a free man.

"I'm so glad they're going to right the wrong they've done to him. He's going to be thrilled."

"Well, this is a start. Next thing we have to do is get that man the restitution that is rightfully his."

"I hope he gets everything he deserves."

Larry laughed. "That's the plan. Give Adam the good news for me and tell him I'll be in touch as soon as I can."

"I'm going to let him know as soon as I can. He's going to be so happy."

Shoving her phone back into her pocket, Sarah quickly went back to the monitor. Larry had gone above and beyond in sending her documentation. Sarah knew that in addition to sending her the information, he'd already sent it to the warden and Adam's public defender

THE LAST HOMESTEAD

as well. By Monday evening, Adam would be walking out of prison for the last time. Her heart started to race as she opened the attached document and instantly started to print it. Sarah had only ever felt so torn once before in her life. That had been five years before when she'd moved from Maine to Florida.

Everything inside of her wanted to stay close to home, but she had to get out and see the world, finding her own path as she went. Florida had been the perfect place to settle down for a while. It was an easy drive up the coast to get to her parents' place, she was close to the ocean she loved, and the warm weather was a blessing that made her miss Maine less. Why had she formed a friendship with the prisoner? She hated that he was going to be gone from her life but found elation in his freedom. Sarah knew Adam had a right to know he would soon be free.

The outdated printer in the back corner roared to life. As it started to print out the first of over forty pages, she leaned back in her chair and closed her eyes. Everything was changing now. It almost seemed befitting, with the solar shower set to start in the next few hours. The event, a rarity for the globe as a whole, had brought to light the shortcomings the planet had taken for such an event. While the forecast had been pinpointed for days to a select few areas, it didn't mean everyone wasn't on high alert.

Grabbing her phone, Sarah had one more call to make before she told Adam the good news. Becky was working at the hospital and had once again sent her home with an amazing meal. The woman took her lunch at the same time as her husband, Alan. They would be finishing up, and Sarah wanted to thank her for being so wonderful. Sarah dialed her friend's number, and she answered right away.

"Hello, Sarah. Did Alan give you the spaghetti I sent with him?"

"He sure did. Again, thank you so much for being such a wonderful person."

"You don't have to thank me. Between you and Alan, I don't have too many other people who mean that much. Plus, I need to make sure my best friend is eating properly."

"Well, you're doing a fine job of it so far," Sarah said. "How's everything going for you today?"

"Another day in crazy town." Becky chuckled. "Everyone is freaking out about this solar storm that's supposed to come through, and we've been packed ever since I walked through the door."

"I can only imagine how many people are going nuts out there. At least it's quiet here at the prison."

"It's easy to keep calm when you're locked in a cell for the majority of the day. Hell, just give them a sedative if they start freaking out. Let them sleep it away."

Sarah laughed. "Don't get me wrong, there are days I wish I could knock the majority of them out for a few hours."

"I bet. Say, are you coming to the cookout on Thursday?" Becky asked.

"I damn near forgot, but I'll be there."

"I can't wait to see you. Just make sure my husband gets home tonight. I'd really like to see him, too."

"Oh, your man will be home. Come a blackout or not, he's going to be coming home."

"Good, then you have nothing to worry about."

Sarah chuckled. "Anyway. I need to get some things done around here, but I just wanted to thank you for dinner and see how your day was going."

"Well, you're very welcome, and I hope you have a good night."

Ending the call, she slipped her phone back into her pocket and listened to the printer as it hummed behind her. How the ancient beast was still alive, Sarah had no idea. For years she'd been asking the budget committee to replace it. Now, knowing that the instant it was done, she'd have to go show Adam, Sarah prayed for the old beast to break down. While she was happy he was going to be released, there was a part of her that wasn't ready for the man to go. When the printer stopped of its own accord and beeped to signal it was done, her heart ached.

"Damn," she muttered.

Despite wanting to wait a little while longer, Sarah had never been one to drag out the inevitable. When it came to breaking up with her past boyfriends, she had done so in an effective and well-thought-out manner. They could say she was cold, but Sarah didn't see it that way. She hated herself for making the comparison between past relationships and what she had with Adam. It was apples to oranges. As she stood and stretched out, Sarah closed her eyes and drew a deep breath. Suddenly, everything around her plunged into darkness.

6

Her eyes shot open, and Sarah's hands instinctively moved to her weapon and flashlight. The entire block had been plunged into darkness. An eerie silence encompassed her. The generators would kick on at any minute. Grabbing her flashlight, she flicked it several times before remembering it wouldn't work if they'd been hit with an EMP. Sarah groaned. There would be supplies in the storage room that were protected, but it would be a pain to navigate in the dark. Still, they couldn't spend the night fumbling through the dark.

She fished around in her pocket and pulled out the lighter she kept on hand for her one addiction, cigarettes. It was a terrible habit Sarah despised herself for having. Now the little flicker of light made it possible for her to move to the landing and down the steps without breaking her neck. Some of the inmates who struggled to sleep were now awake. You couldn't miss the complete lack of noise that emanated from the world around them. Even in the dead of night, there was a hum to the facility as old as Glenwood.

Now there was nothing. Somewhere in the distance, she could hear the clipping of Alan's shoes moving down the hall in her direction. She headed for the common room, where all guards met in the event of an emergency. It bothered her that the generators hadn't kicked in yet. Even the emergency backup lights that would normally give off a dim glow appeared to be on the fritz.

Cursing under her breath, she thought about the pack of smokes in her purse upstairs and wished she'd grabbed them. As soon as the others realized what was happening, they'd join her in the block's common room. Until then, they needed to figure out what was going on with the generators. Alan appeared relieved when she met him in the common area.

"What in the hell is going on right now?" Alan asked. "The power is out, and the phones are dead, too."

"I think it's just a matter of the solar storm. The effects of the EMP must have gone out farther than the government predicted. It's not often that our scientists get something like this wrong, but it's not impossible. Everything is down now."

"I know they have things in place in case something like this happens, but what are we supposed to do now?"

"For now, I want you to stay right here and wait for the others. I need to do a walkthrough and a count of the inmates."

"You're going to do a count right now? Shouldn't you wait for the others first before doing that?"

"Normally, we would. The problem is that the protocol calls for a count, and I need you to wait for everyone else to get here," Sarah said. "Now, I'm going to walk the block, and you're going to wait for me to get back before doing anything."

"Okay. Just promise me you'll be careful."

"I promise, but you have nothing to worry about yet. I figure they'll have us back up and running soon. Won't even be enough time for the inmates to get riled up."

"Sure, that's easy for you to say." Alan laughed. "I'd imagine there are more than a few of these guys who would like to get their hands on you."

"Not today," Sarah said. "Anyway, is Becky still at work?"

"Well, she was heading home when I got off the phone with her. I'm sure she's made her way to the house by now."

"Good. I'm sure it's going to get even crazier now that the power and everything else are out. I'll be back here shortly."

The lighter had cooled since she'd used it to navigate the hall leading to the common room. Now that she was moving through the halls again, she needed the dim light to do a head count. The men hated it, and she did her best to let them keep sleeping, but she couldn't spend all night on it. She gave each inmate ten seconds. If she couldn't see them breathing beneath the sheets, Sarah tapped on the bars to get them to stir. As she moved from one cell to the next, keeping a mental tally in her head, she saw a familiar arm hanging out two cells ahead and grinned.

It was John. When he saw her coming, he drew his arms back inside the cell. While Sarah trusted him beyond measure, she appreciated that he always followed protocol. It kept the less-trusted inmates from asking questions and trying to push the rules. He looked relieved when he saw her. Sarah was one of the few people who knew how much John feared the dark. If she had a spare lighter and the authority to give it to him, then she would have in a heartbeat. His fear stemmed from a traumatizing boat ride in the hull of an illegal ship to the coast of Florida as a child. The trip had taken his parents' lives.

With the lighter again burning her thumb, she let the flame die out as she paused by John's door. She hated that John was alone in the dark, and there was nothing she could do. They had to get to the flashlights in their protective cases, buried in storage.

"How are you holding up, John?" Sarah asked.

"Oh, I'll be doing a lot better when the lights come on. That much, I can tell you for sure."

Sarah chuckled. "I thought you wanted to break up the monotony. I'd venture to say that this should have done it for you."

"You're not wrong, but I'd still prefer the lights to be on. Besides, it's just not the same when you're locked in a cage, and there's no power."

"I understand. I'm sure they're going to get everything back up and running before too long."

"Still don't have any idea how long it's going to be or what caused it?" John asked.

"I think the solar storm hit a larger area than they were expecting. As for a time frame on how long it's going to take, I have nothing but bad news. Just hold tight, and they'll get us back up and going again."

"Imagine that. The scientists and the news got their information wrong. I never would have guessed that could happen."

Sarah laughed. "Yeah. I think I'm with you on that one, but I definitely expected them to be better with figuring this thing out."

"See, that's the problem with the government right now. They have their heads so far up their asses that they can't see what's right in front of them," John said.

"Hey, now. It's not all that bad."

"No, but I got myself into this cage for the things I've done, and I think plenty of government officials should be right here beside me."

"I can't say I disagree with that. For now, you just

relax, and we'll get all of this figured out before too long." Sarah smiled. "I'll keep you posted if I hear anything."

"Thank you," John replied.

Sarah would be breaking the rules for John, a decision she'd made as soon as she'd seen the man's terrified expression. Once she had the flashlights in hand, she would slip one into John's cell. The man had served his time and deserved a few perks. Plus, it was a blackout. All she was doing was making sure all of her inmates were safe physically and mentally. John needed the flashlight for his mental health, and Sarah trusted him with it. Moving to the end of the hall, she continued her count until she reached the end.

Everyone was present and accounted for, not that she'd expected anything different. Twenty minutes had passed since the lights had gone out. In the stillness of the night, Sarah could hear the doors on the far end of the block opening and knew the others were coming to gather in the common area. She quickly jogged back to the main room just as figures started to emerge from the hall. It was good to see them all congregating. A half dozen of them had lighters just like her to guide the way.

She was certain Harden would have a few choice words for those with the banned lighters, but it was something they could deal with later. At that moment, they needed to find out how long the lights were going to stay off. Harden had joined the others in the common room. She handed out long white candles with paper bases to keep the wax off their hands. Sarah had no idea where their commanding officer had gotten them, but she was happy the woman was prepared. They went around lighting the candles and getting settled before Harden cleared her throat.

For the first time, Sarah saw the panicked look in her eyes.

7

"All right, everyone, settle down. As you've all figured out by now, we were hit with an EMP," Harden said.

"Not that we aren't thrilled that you're here, boss, but it's a little early for your shift, isn't it?" Alan asked.

She smiled at him. "I have a stack of paperwork on my desk that doesn't care about the nine-to-five hours. Plus, I wanted to be here in case something like this happened. It's a good thing I did, too, not that I don't trust you all."

"So, what's the plan, Cap?" Sarah asked.

"We've got a procedure in place for power outages. It doesn't look like the boxes protected the generators. In addition, many of you have noticed your phones and flashlights aren't working, either. The morning shift will be here in two hours. When they arrive, we'll start getting this sorted out."

Sarah listened as the captain started laying out what they would do for the next few hours. As much as they wanted to wait it out, there were still things that had to be done. A handful of the men imprisoned at the facility needed medications that would have to be logged by hand. They were going to have to work together as a team to make sure everything got done. Thankfully, in a few hours, they would have relief on the way, along with a team of people to get the power restored.

The morning shift would have to work double time to get meals out. If asked, Sarah had no problem with staying on longer to help out. The extra cash would help cover the six weeks she'd be without a paycheck in the fall. Turning her attention back to the captain, Sarah listened as she spoke. One day, Sarah wanted to be the one running things, and Harden was an amazing leader to learn from.

"They should already have relief teams en route, and the first shift crew will be here at their normal times. Until then, we're on lockdown."

"How long will the facility be on lockdown?" one of the officers asked.

"For now, it's going to be this way at least until the morning count. I don't want to take any chances of something getting out of hand."

"What about the electronics being down? We have no way to contact anyone or get information from the state."

"Look, I don't have any more information than any of you have. As far as I know, they are sorting out the problem. I have no idea how long it's going to take or when we will be back online. Until then, we follow protocol. Don't do anything outside of the normal procedures that have been set in place."

Sarah knew things would be difficult without the power, but she had no idea how long they'd be able to sustain a healthy environment for the inmates in their care. Still, it surprised her that there were so many questions from the other staff members. For the most part, it didn't matter what the situation was. There were things in place to take care of any situation. She continued to listen to Harden as she spoke to the group and answered questions. Suddenly, one of the officers came in from another block.

"None of the cars have any power. It doesn't look like any of us are getting out of here anytime soon."

The group of officers started to mumble amongst themselves. Sarah still wasn't bothered much by the situation. If there was anything her parents taught her had stuck, it was the idea to be prepared for anything. It was interesting to hear how Harden handled everything. She felt lucky to have a strong woman to learn from if she was to ever take over the same position.

"Anything I hear, I'll pass along at morning roll call. We have a few hours until then, so I need each of you to get back to your posts. Work doesn't stop, even if it is the end of the world." Harden smiled.

As they all started to part ways and head back to their blocks, Sarah thought about the stalled cars in the lots. It was strange that such a powerful hit was isolated. She was curious to learn how far out it went, but the questions would have to wait for the relief shift to come. It was infuriating that the government had gotten the location of the solar storm hitting so incredibly wrong. It wasn't that much of a surprise, given how often they screwed up. Watching the group move away, Sarah headed for Adam's cell. In the chaos, she hadn't been able to tell Adam what she had learned about his case.

There was no way any of the prisoners were still sleeping after the posse of guards moved through. She wanted to go right to his cell and tell him the good news, but before she could, Alan grabbed her arm. The captain and one of the other guards were still in the common room. Her heart raced. Alan had known where she was going and had protected her. If the captain knew how fond she was of Adam, there would be consequences. At the very least, it would be a written note in her file, and that was something her budding career couldn't take.

Smiling at her friend and silently thanking him, she quickly headed back to the common room to see if the captain needed anything else. The last thing she wanted was to appear like she was lingering around and doing nothing. It didn't take long for the guard to leave the captain, and Meredith turned to Sarah. She gave the woman an exhausted head shake as she approached Sarah. For the first time since starting at Glenwood, Sarah noticed a fatigued look in her boss's eyes.

"Sarah, how are you holding up with all of this going on?"

"I'm doing all right. I just want the power to come back on or the morning sun to give us some light." Sarah chuckled.

"It shouldn't be much longer now. I think we're about an hour away from the sun shining through all these windows. It will be a lot better when it does," Meredith said. "How's your block doing?"

"They're all doing pretty well, for the most part. I still need to get down to the storage room and get the flashlights."

"I wouldn't even bother wasting your time on that. All the other blocks have already grabbed the flashlights, and there isn't a single one that works. Whatever this solar storm contained, it seemed to do a number on anything electrical."

"Well, shit," Sarah muttered.

Meredith laughed. "I know this isn't the ideal thing you wanted to hear, but we're going to get through this. We've got a protocol for the power outage, and I'm sure they're working on this situation as we speak."

"Sure, not going to make our job any easier until they get it fixed. Still, I'm sure they'll get it all figured out."

"They will. Just keep your chin up and follow what we're supposed to do. It will be light out soon, and everything will be a lot smoother when it is."

Meredith turned and walked away. Sarah tried to think of a plan to help some of the inmates, but she hated that there was nothing she could do for John. It was one thing to give him a flashlight, but it was a termination-level offense to give an inmate a lit candle. She couldn't risk her job, but the sun would be coming up soon, and the light would filter in. As she watched Harden leave out the far doors, Sarah headed for Adam's cell. The time had come for him to learn that he would soon be a free man. She drew a breath to steady herself, knowing it was wrong for her to be procrastinating.

Adam deserved his freedom. Hopefully, he would be able to get compensation from the government for being wrongly imprisoned. The chances of that happening were relatively good, considering it had been crooked officers who had put him behind bars to start with. She wanted to be happy for her friend, but it was still a bittersweet moment as she approached his cell. Just as she'd suspected, he was still awake and sitting at the end of his bunk. The light from the candle gave away her approach.

He stood and smiled at her, making her heart race once again. Sarah hated herself for having feelings for the man. They confused and upset her. There was no way that she was going to tell him or anyone else how she truly felt. Her job was everything to her. Sharing how she felt would only create more confusion for Adam. He didn't deserve that after ten years of being unfairly institutionalized. As Adam approached the bars, Sarah forced herself to smile at him and bury the feelings deep down. With any luck, they would stay there.

8

"It's been a long shift, huh?" Adam asked.

"You're telling me," Sarah grumbled. "I've never seen anything like it. Everything fried, even the cars."

He gave a low whistle and shook his head. "I guess that means no morning news. That's a shame. I'm sure the media is going to have a field day with this."

"A prison without power? You better believe it," Sarah said.

She knew she had to tell him about his case. It was ridiculous that she was still procrastinating. With everything going on at the prison, could anyone really blame her for not making it a priority? He wouldn't care about their daily conversations when he had his freedom knocking at the door. It wasn't like her to hold on to things so tightly. The way Adam was looking at her, she didn't want to tell him anything.

He had the ability to know what was in her soul without her saying a single word. It was both infuriating and confusing. No matter what happened after he got out of prison, he still had a reputation that she couldn't risk tangling herself in with a former convict, no matter how innocent he might be.

"What's on your mind, Sarah? I can tell you're thinking hard about something," Adam said. "Is the captain getting on your case about the power outage?"

"No, nothing like that. So, far, she's been pretty good about everything we're dealing with."

"Well, that's good. At least she's not jumping down your throat. Tell me, what is going on?"

"It's an email that I received a little bit ago that the prosecutor sent over."

"What do you mean?" Adam asked. "Is everything okay with the family?"

Sarah sighed. "It's got nothing to do with me or my family. I'm actually friends with the prosecutor. We've known each other for quite some time, and he keeps me posted on several ongoing cases."

"Sounds like we're going to be getting some new people here soon."

"Well, crime doesn't stop, and this is the place they send them." Sarah chuckled nervously. "I'm sure we'll have new inmates soon, but that's not what he was emailing me about."

"Whatever it is, it seems to have you knotted up. So, tell me what this email was about."

Sarah was still struggling to tell the man he was finally going to get to go home. She couldn't help but think that things were going to be different as soon as he left. Adam had become more than just a routine and a good part of her day. There was something more to what she was feeling, but none of that mattered. It was his life, and he deserved to live it how he saw fit.

"The prosecutor has been keeping in touch with me about your case," Sarah said.

"What did he say about it?"

"The judge signed off on everything. You're going to be cleared of all charges, and come Monday morning, you're going to be a free man. We just have to wait for them to send the paperwork over before we can release you."

She could see he was blown away by the revelation. He stumbled backward and sat down on his bunk, a dazed look in his eyes. Sarah was overwhelmed with happiness for her friend. Still, she couldn't shake the sadness deep inside of her. It was one thing to be happy for him but another altogether to stand there and try to fake enjoyment.

"I can't believe it," he stammered.

Sarah smiled at him. "You deserve your freedom, Adam. It's long overdue. What they did to you wasn't right."

"Thanks. I can't tell you how much I appreciate everything you've done for me and my case. I know you've gone above and beyond what your job called for."

"I have a problem with people being wrongfully imprisoned. I would do the same for anyone else."

"So, I'm not special, huh?" he asked playfully.

Instantly, a flush jumped to her cheeks as she turned away from him. Sarah didn't want Adam to see just how much his words affected her. He was incredibly special to her, far more than he should have been.

The sun was slowly starting to rise in the sky, but it did nothing to fix the eerie silence that still filled the halls. Something in her gut told her there was more going on outside, but she couldn't leave her job until the relief team came.

Though as more time passed, she was less sure that she was going to stay on after her shift ended. The prison was only a few miles away from town. If the power outage had affected the surrounding area, she wanted to make sure her apartment was safe and secure. It wasn't that she lived in a bad neighborhood, but Sarah knew how desperate people could become in trying times. There was no reason to risk her home being broken into. Turning her attention back to Adam, Sarah smiled at him. She was still his friend no matter what.

"So, I guess asking you what you're going to do when you're free hits a little different now, huh?" Sarah said.

He chuckled and nodded. "Yeah, I guess so. I honestly have no idea what I'm going to do with myself. It's been so long since I was on the outside. I can't imagine how much things have changed."

"Something tells me you are going to adjust just fine," Sarah said.

"Yeah, as long as I steer clear from anything involving the police or government."

"Unfortunately, I think you're right about that. Just remember that not all law enforcement is bad," Sarah said. "You mentioned earlier that you had family in Argentina. You still think you'll head down there and be with them?"

"Well, maybe eventually," Adam replied.

"What do you mean?" Sarah asked. "I thought you'd want to get out of this place as soon as possible."

"I do want to leave here, but for now, I think I'm just going to stick around here for a while."

"After everything this place did to you, why would you want to stick around here?"

"Even if this place royally screwed me over, I didn't really get the chance to see much of Florida. I figure this will give me a chance to see what she has to offer. Maybe make some new friends along the way."

Sarah blushed. "There's not really much of Florida to see. What you can find here is already in the brochure, and they make sure they get every inch of beauty in those things."

Adam chuckled. "Yeah, you're probably right. I really don't know what I'm going to do, but hanging around here and seeing how great Florida can be sounds like my best-case scenario right now."

"Well, the one thing I can tell you for sure is that there

isn't anything great about Florida. I've been here long enough to tell you that much."

"If you can be that sure about something, then I can be sure there's at least one pretty good thing about sticking around."

Sarah didn't know what to say to him as she turned away once again. The next shift of workers would be in soon, and her night was coming to a close. After wishing her friend farewell, Sarah headed for the steps that led to the crow's nest. There was nothing else she could do for him until power was restored. It was strange to be isolated in the facility, not knowing how far the EMP had reached or the amount of damage it had done. All she wanted was to get out of there and hit the open road for a little bit. Driving always made her feel better.

In that instant, she remembered what the guard from B block had told them earlier. None of the cars were starting. They would be stranded there until the others arrived. Sarah was starting to feel the fatigue of the shift as she sat down. There wasn't much to do without the power on. All of her paperwork required the internet or, at the very least, some light to complete. She hated having idle time to kill. There had to be something she could do. The facility was massive, after all. Sarah hated being paid for sitting on her rear.

A quick glance at the clock on the wall told her it wasn't working. It was the strangest thing that everything around them had died. The EMP must have been more powerful than they were anticipating. It drove her nuts, but the backup generators hadn't kicked in yet. How were they supposed to do their jobs and keep the inmates safe when they couldn't even use the restrooms? It was those questions, along with the onslaught of others, that kept her mind buzzing as she waited.

9

Without any way to tell time, Sarah made her way to the main doors when she suspected it was close to the time the day shift would be arriving. With the security panels that unlocked the doors through key cards down, someone needed to be at the entrance to let the next shift in. She was a little surprised to see that no one was waiting at the doors for her when she opened them. The hot Florida sun poured into the prison block. They should have been starting to arrive minutes ago. It bothered her that everyone seemed to be running late.

Sarah knew some of the correction officers and other employees lived in town, though, and the EMP might have made coming to work impossible. Still, at least a handful of employees lived over twenty miles away from the facility. They should have been there for the morning shift, yet the only cars in the parking lot were those that had sat there all night. The sense of foreboding returned to her once more. It seemed like something more was going on. She frowned and headed back into the cell block to find Alan.

The others would be gathering soon for the morning roll call, and she didn't want to miss it. With Adam now aware of his situation, she had nothing left there to keep her around. Sarah wanted to get out of there and fast. With the light flooding in through the windows perched near the roof, she no longer needed the candle burning in her hand. Blowing it out, she quickly set it down and gathered her bag. Sarah yawned and stretched out. Who knew what kind of chaos they would be dealing with for the next few days.

There was a knock on her office door, and she quickly glanced up. Alan smiled at her and waved from the other side. Sarah motioned for him to come in and join her.

"How's everything going out there?" Sarah asked.

"Oh, you know. Nothing but complaining from most of the inmates. Plus, not having any of the answers to their questions is a pain in the ass."

Sarah chuckled. "Well, that's just something else we're going to have to work through. I'm sure they'll have all of this figured out in no time. Until then, we just have to make do with what we have."

"Not as easy as it sounds," Alan replied. "Hey, did you happen to give Adam the good news? I'm hoping he's excited to finally get out of here and get on with his life."

"I did tell him. I don't think he quite understands what it means just yet, but I could tell he was glad to finally leave."

"I'm happy for him. Just so you know, the captain is here along with the others. They've all been here for about half an hour now."

"Good. I was starting to worry that the relief team wasn't going to make it in. With none of the cars having any power, along with nothing else, it seems, I didn't know if we would all get any relief."

"Unfortunately, you're still right. The captain is here along with some others who have been here."

"What do you mean that I'm right?" Sarah asked. "I thought you just said that the others were here. Are we not getting any relief?"

"Well, at the moment, we haven't had a single member of the relief team show up. Also, there's absolutely no way of getting ahold of any of them, either."

"So, not one person has come in yet?"

"Not a one of them. I don't know what we're going to do, but the captain is waiting to talk to all of us."

Sarah frowned and headed out the door after Alan. Just as he'd said, the only people in the common room were the ones she'd seen hours earlier when they'd met to do a roll call. Meredith looked more worried than she had hours before. It was easy to understand why, though, since no one had shown up for work. They couldn't leave the facility unattended. Until reinforcements came, they would all be stuck at the prison.

From the way things were going, it looked like Sarah was going to get her overtime anyway. Her mind raced as she pondered what the lack of relief workers meant. Given the circumstances outside, it was entirely possible that the county officials had placed the general public under a state of emergency. If that were indeed the case, the only people on the roads would be members of the military and police force. Still, special privileges could be granted to prison personnel if Meredith had any way of contacting them.

The mood was noticeably different than it had been hours before. People were worried. She listened as the group whispered amongst themselves. Several of the guards had gone out to the parking lot to work on their vehicles, but none had been successful in getting them started. From one trio of employees, she could hear the whispers of an uprising taking root. They didn't want to be there. They had families they needed to check on. She could understand their fears and silently thanked God that her parents were safely in Maine, where they had power. Still, something had to be done to calm the group. They had a job to do.

"All right, everyone. Get settled in," Meredith said. "I have some things we need to go over. The sooner we get through this, the sooner we can get back to figuring out what we need to do."

The conversations taking place throughout the group quickly quieted. It was always interesting to see how fast her coworkers followed the captain's lead. Once everyone was settled in and had their attention on Meredith, the woman cleared her throat and started to speak to the group.

"Okay. So, as you all know, we have no communication. That goes for everyone in here, along with the outside world. I hate to be the one who has to tell you all, but we're going to have to get started on the morning routine. We are the day shift as of right now."

"Has there been any new information?" a guard asked.

"As I said, there has been no new communication, and the radios are still down. I don't have anything new to tell you."

"How long are we going to be stuck here? Some of us have families we need to check on."

"I understand you all have questions, and I wish I had the answers, but I don't. I have no idea when anyone will come in."

"What about sending someone into town to get some news? I think we can handle one guard going and finding something out."

Meredith sighed. "It's something I've already been planning on doing. Sending just one person out to get news for us all seems like the best solution right now."

"Who are you going to send?" the guard asked.

"I was going to ask if anyone wants to volunteer to go."

Sarah's hand was the only one that didn't shoot into the air. As much as she wanted to go out and explore like the rest of them, she knew her skills were of better use to

Meredith at the facility. Looking around at the other guards, she struggled to think of one of them making the trek into town and back in any reasonable amount of time. The only other employee in good shape was Michael Cook, a secondary guard from A block, but he had a cast on his leg from a motorcycle accident the month before.

With the town of Glenwood just over two miles away, Sarah knew she could get there and back in roughly thirty minutes. The others would take at least two hours round trip. Her eyes scanned the group once more before moving back to their leader standing on a bench above them. Harden was already looking at Sarah. She cringed and slowly raised her hand to offer up her services, knowing it was what their boss was waiting for. Instantly, Meredith called her name, and the others grumbled disapprovingly around her.

After a long and harrowing shift, she understood just how much they all wanted to get a brief respite from the prison, but it was still work time. Sarah would do what she was sent out to accomplish and be back as quickly as possible. The inmates would start to get restless soon. Their doors should have opened a half hour before to start the morning rounds, but the cells were still safely locked with the inmates inside. It would take the skeleton crew hours just to get everyone fed and out for a little while. She had to move fast.

10

"Are you sure this is a good idea? I know Craig or Mike would take longer, but I don't feel right leaving you here to fend for yourself," Sarah said.

Meredith chuckled. "Trust me, if I thought any of the others could get there and back in under two hours, I'd consider it. Just find out what you can, try to get ahold of the commissioner, and get back here."

"Right," Sarah muttered.

She already had the commissioner's phone number tucked into the breast pocket of her uniform. Harden's orders were clear. Sarah was to go directly to the police station and let the officers know the prison was without power. From there, she would go to the bakery on Main Street and buy out their breakfast foods for the inmates and guards alike. Without power, they had limited options for meals. Meredith was an amazing captain, though, and hadn't hesitated to spend the money needed to keep everyone placated. They were a team, and Meredith wasn't going to let anything happen to her prison in Sarah's absence.

Still, it was hard to leave the compound, knowing they had no way to reach the outside world. Any number of things could go wrong in the hour she was absent. Sarah couldn't let the never-ending list of what-ifs cloud her mind. There was only one task she could focus on at that moment, and the others were just slowing her down. She had to keep her head clear and her mind sharp. There would be people in the area who were still without power. While she'd normally give everyone around her the benefit of the doubt, it was a tense situation where caution had to be paramount above everything else.

"Just make sure you're safe out there," Meredith said. "There's no telling what kind of reaction the people are going to have in a situation like this. Keep an eye out for danger on the road, too."

"I'll get there and back as quickly as I can. Don't forget that I have training in martial arts."

"I'd rather you not have to use your knowledge in hand-to-hand combat if you don't have to. Just keep an eye out and don't let anything happen to yourself."

"Well, if push comes to shove, I always have my gun on me as well," Sarah said.

Meredith laughed. "Just keep in mind that a single clip won't stop an angry mob of people. We have no idea what's going on out there, and I only want to make sure you get back here safely."

"I'll do the best I can. I just want to get some kind of information about what in the hell is going on out there and get back here to let you know."

"Good. If you would like me to send a second person with you, I can do that. All you have to do is say the word."

For a moment, Sarah thought about telling her that it would be nice to go with another person. Meredith was right about one thing—they had no idea how people were reacting to the power being out. In a perfect world, people would just be helping one another through the hard times, but having been in the "rehabilitation" business as long as she had, she knew the dark side of people better than she cared to admit.

"I think I'll manage better on my own," Sarah said. "It will be faster that way. Just hold the fort down, and I'll be back before you start handing out the morning medications."

"All right, just be safe."

As Sarah made her way to the main doors that led to the enclosed courtyard connecting the four blocks, she glanced at Adam's cell. He was sitting on his bunk and smiled when he saw her. Sarah knew Meredith was watching her go and couldn't stop. Instead, she gave him a small wave and continued down the corridor. She unlocked the door and stepped out into the blinding sun.

Instantly, what little coolness the building had retained from the night was gone, and she felt the familiar beads of sweat that came with Florida life rolling down the small of her back.

Sarah paused and waved at the guard stationed at the outside tower. He'd been at roll call with all the others and thus had been expecting Sarah to appear eventually. Stretching out, she prepared herself for the pending jog before trotting to the second set of locked gates near the main road and staff parking lot. Even in the secluded location, she felt like something was off. It was far too quiet outside. The usual roar of the highway a few miles north didn't fill the air. Instead, only the sounds of nature greeted her as she locked the gates behind herself and looked down the two-lane road.

She had changed into her tennis shoes and workout clothing for the run. The only thing Sarah kept with her was the weapon registered in her name and the button-up shirt she wore as a uniform at the compound. Clipped to the pocket was her staff identification card, and in the zipped pocket on the right, it had the commissioner's number and her wallet. Normally, she would take a backpack or shoulder pouch while running, but she'd planned on using the staff gym instead of running after her shift ended. Caught off guard, Sarah had to make do with what she had on hand.

After she managed to get her stride, the run went smoothly. Despite the fact that she smoked, running seemed to counterbalance her nasty habit, and she didn't get easily winded. Sarah listened and watched for any signs of other travelers, but there were none. As she moved closer to town, cars littered the road. Some were alone in the middle of the street, and others were still smoldering from crashes that had occurred hours before. The sinking sensation in her stomach only grew as the village came into view. She had expected to see signs of power by the time she reached it, yet the only noises that greeted her were humans and nature. She slowed when she reached the main road that housed the sheriff's station.

The door was standing open, yet no gust of air conditioning or the buzz of electronics greeted her. Instead, a lone officer sat at the reception desk, frantically scribbling notes on a pad of paper. He jumped when he heard her walk in and clear her throat. The man looked frazzled as if he hadn't slept in days. He took one look at the gun on her hip and the uniform in her hands and instantly sprang to his feet.

"What can I do for you, Officer?"

"I'm not police. I'm a corrections officer at the prison down the road. My name is Sarah Fowler, and I need to get in touch with the commissioner. The power is out at the prison, and none of our relief has shown up. We're going to need some backup."

The man stood silent for several moments like the words she had spoken went right through him. Sarah watched him and waited for the man to say something, but he only looked at her dumbfounded. She wasn't sure how to take him, but there were a million questions she needed answers to, and he didn't seem as if he was going to answer any of them.

"Look, we've been out of power since late last night. How far did the EMP hit?" Sarah asked.

A shocked look rushed over the man's face. "You haven't heard?"

"What in the hell are you talking about? We've had no communication since the power went down. I just assumed the solar storm knocked out a portion of the state's power."

"Well, you're in for a surprise then. The storm was a lot bigger than they ever expected. In fact, it was massive."

"How big are we talking? Is the whole state of Florida in the dark now?"

"I don't think it's just the state," the man said. "I'm starting to think the whole nation has been rocked by the storm. If not the country, then most of the world. I wouldn't be surprised if everyone on the planet was in the dark about how bad it was. Even things that run off batteries don't work."

The world around her started to spin as she struggled to wrap her mind around what the man was telling her. Instantly, her thoughts raced to her parents on their homestead in Maine. They weren't safe anymore. No one was. She wanted to run from the station and not stop until she reached her parents' property but as quickly as the thought struck her, Sarah shut it back down. If she stood any chance of making it back home, she had to be prepared, and that meant getting back to the prison first. The others had to know.

11

"I have to get back to the prison and tell my captain," Sarah stammered.

"Really? No offense, but it's kind of every man for himself right now. This shit isn't going to blow over. Everything is fried. No electronics at all. No coffee makers, no phones, no cable, no—"

"I get it," she growled. "You're the only one here. Do you really want three hundred-plus inmates taking over your town?"

His face paled.

"That's what I thought," Sarah snapped.

There was no point in sticking around to argue with the man. Whatever he was doing was for the community's good, and she needed to get back to her own people. For now, keeping the inmates locked up was their only option. Sarah was unsure of how long that plan could stay in place. Once news got out to the other guards that the entire world had been plunged into darkness, there was no telling if they would stick around. Heck, Sarah had no intentions of staying longer than she absolutely needed to.

Her parents would always be her first concern. She turned back and started for the road again, with the officer still calling after her. There was no reason for her to stay and chat with the man, not with the information she'd learned. The trip back took half the time of the one into town. Knowing what she knew now, Sarah could feel a pressing sense of urgency with each passing minute. Her parents were good people and wouldn't hesitate to help out anyone who crossed their land, and that was what worried her most.

In desperate times, people could become monsters. She wasn't going to let her parents fall victim to the creatures that havoc could raise. As she breathlessly reached the front gates, her hands shook as she fumbled with the keys. Before long, she was back in her cell block but didn't immediately go to the crow's nest, where she knew Meredith was waiting. Her first instinct had been to go to the storage room, but she'd quickly become distracted. Now, she needed to see what resources were available.

It was roughly thirteen hundred miles to get to her parents' place on the Maine and New Hampshire border. The trip would take her at least twelve days by foot if she was able to keep moving at a quick pace. Despite her hopes that the entire nation hadn't been hit, Sarah could feel in her gut that the police officer had been telling her the truth. Making her way down the dark steps that led to the basement, she reached the locked door and flicked her lighter to life to find the right key. Before long, she was looking through the shelves and filling a book bag.

She wouldn't dream of taking the supplies without Meredith's approval, but Sarah had no misconceptions about what was going to transpire. Once word got out that the whole world was dark, no one would be okay with sticking around to run the prison. What was the point of keeping the men locked away when eventually the food would run out, and they'd all starve to death in their cells? Sarah shuddered and thanked God it wasn't a decision that rested on her shoulders. Grabbing two extra gun clips and three boxes of ammo, she slipped back out of the basement and up the steps.

Seconds later, as she stepped into her crow's nest, Sarah set the bag on the floor and looked at Meredith. As soon as the woman saw the look in Sarah's eyes, her face paled. Meredith Harden hadn't gotten to her position by not learning to read people. The woman swallowed.

"I'm going to take it that you didn't find anything good out there?"

"From what the officer said at the station, it's every man for themselves. He thinks it's not just Florida but the whole world that has been thrown into darkness," Sarah said. "It's not looking good for anyone right now."

"Oh my God," Meredith replied, looking down at the bag Sarah had packed. "Are you leaving?"

"I can give this a few days. I don't want to leave you in a situation like this. After a couple of days, if nothing changes—"

"I understand. Your parents are going to need you."

"I'm sorry, Meredith. I don't really have a choice in the matter. I can't imagine how the world is going to react, but I know my parents are going to take in anyone looking for help without asking questions."

"There's no need to explain yourself. Family is always going to come first, and I'm just glad you're willing to give me a little of your time before you leave. I'm going to need all the help I can get here, but I can't make you stay any more than the rest of the staff."

"I'll help as much as I can before then," Sarah said.

"I appreciate it."

"What are we going to do right now?"

"The first thing we need to do is get all the guards together and explain what is going on out there. I can only assume that you're not going to be the only one wanting to leave. I just hope a few of them decide to stick around."

"I'll go find Alan. We'll meet you in the common room shortly."

"Thank you, Sarah. It's going to get a lot worse before it gets any better," Meredith said.

"Trust me, I know."

Looking down at the common room below, a sense of

dread filled Sarah. She didn't like the idea of the inmates overhearing the news she'd just shared with her captain. All it took was one person listening in on the conversation and the news would spread through the inmate's cells like wildfire. They'd find themselves in a dangerous situation. Everything had to be handled carefully. She didn't know how many guards would still be there when the news broke. Her stomach lurched. The moment of hesitation drew Meredith's attention.

"What's going through your mind?" Meredith asked.

"I don't think it's a good idea to meet in the commons room."

"What do you mean?"

"Once any of the inmates figure out what is going on, it's going to be a mess. I think we should meet outside and tell everyone the news there."

Meredith sighed. "I didn't think about it like that. Good call. Listen, I know all hell is going to break loose once word gets around to the inmates here. I don't know what to expect when that happens."

"All I know is that it's going to get bad around here, and I don't think anyone is going to come to relieve us," Sarah said. "I'll let Alan know what's going on, and I'll also get word over to the men in the sentry tower outside. We'll meet you outside."

"Sounds good. I'll get the others together so we can let them know what's happened. I just wish it wasn't such bad news."

"Well, nothing we can do to change that. We just need

to reassure them that staying is the right thing to do for now."

"We can't make them stay. Most of them have families they are going to want to check on."

"I know, but I hope we can come to a group decision on staying."

"Me too. Go get Alan and spread the word about meeting outside," Meredith said. "If I were you, I'd take your bag and lock it in your office. Don't leave it unlocked at any point."

"I'll make sure it's secure," Sarah replied. "Meet you in a few minutes."

"Just be careful, Sarah. For the love of God, be careful. I don't need anything to happen to you."

As Meredith headed down the steps, Sarah tucked her bag beneath the desk before following after her commanding officer. She checked to make sure the door locked behind her. They parted ways at the bottom of the steps as Sarah headed into the bowels of the compound in search of Alan. He deserved to know what was going on. The thought of Becky and the children fending for themselves nearly broke her heart. The news would be devastating to her friend. His wife was no helpless waif. Becky could hold her own and had the ferocity of a protective mother at all times.

She wouldn't let anything happen to her children, but that knowledge would do little to put her friend's mind at rest. Sarah wouldn't hold it against him if he decided to leave. In the same vein of thought, she had to wonder how many others there deserved a fighting chance. John and certainly Adam didn't deserve to die in their cells simply because of who they were in the past. Everything was different now. They all had a fresh slate waiting for them.

12

She didn't hesitate when she saw the storage door open at the end of the hall. It was the second access point to the basement and the only other place she hadn't yet checked for Alan. Still, Sarah was happy he was in a secluded location. He was a devoted family man, and the news that Meredith was about to share with the others would hit him hard. She wanted to tell him beforehand so he could be prepared.

When she found him in the room, he was taking count by candlelight. He smiled when he saw her and stopped scribbling on the notepad in his hands. If he made it three rooms over, he'd find they were short on their stock after what she took. Hopefully, he'd understand why when she told him the truth about what was happening. There was still a hesitation in her. Chaos was going to ensue soon, and there was nothing she could do to prevent it from happening. How were they going to keep three-hundred men locked up?

It would take the government weeks to get the power turned back on at best. More than likely, Sarah knew they were looking at months or potentially years in the same darkness that their ancestors had combated. Unfortunately, they were no longer prepared for the harsh conditions that their predecessors had mastered. People would be dying by the thousands. She couldn't think about the chaos that had befallen the larger cities.

For the first time in years, she was grateful to her parents for insisting she had the skills to defend herself and survive in the harsh wilderness. Her heart broke for those stranded around the world, those who had died in car crashes without knowing what was happening as the power left their vehicles. The airplanes, the boats, the stranded people—she couldn't think about it at that moment. Not when Alan and her parents, along with others like John and Adam, needed her. She had to keep her mind sharp for all of them.

"Well, that doesn't look like the face of someone with good news," Alan said. "What's going on, Sarah?"

"It doesn't sound like anyone in the country has power, and if that's the case, it's going to be a long time before we get any power back on."

"What am I supposed to make of that?"

"It seems like the storm hit harder than anyone imagined. Word has it that it wasn't just Florida that got hit with it. It's literally everywhere."

Alan grew silent.

"Look, I know you're worried about Becky and the kids, but you have to remember how tough your wife is. No matter what she's up against, she'll find a way through it."

"I just don't know what I'm supposed to do," Alan said. "Do I leave here and go find my wife and kids, or do I stay to help here."

"No one is going to give you shit for leaving. You know that, right?" Sarah asked.

"I know, but I hate the thought of leaving when there are so many things to do here. Are we going to get any help at all?"

"Honestly, I doubt it. If they haven't come yet, I'd just rather assume they're not going to at all."

"What about you?" Alan asked. "Have you figured out what you're going to do? I can only imagine you're worried about your parents."

"I am. That's why I'm going to stay and help out here for a couple of days, and then I'm going to go."

"I need to think about this. On the one hand, I know how important it is to stay here. I mean, all these inmates can cause havoc out there."

"Well, before you decide to do anything, we have to go to the courtyard. Meredith wants everyone to gather out there and let us know what's going on."

Sarah led the way through the hall, where the inmates were now growing restless. They yelled at the guards, demanding answers as to what was happening, but neither of them stopped. They would be able to tell the men more as soon as they were done meeting with the others. By the time they reached the courtyard, Meredith and the others were already gathered. She saw the guards from the tower were already with the group as well. Sarah fell in with the rest of the group as they gathered around Meredith. She cleared her throat, but Sarah could tell she was nervous.

"All right, everyone, settle down. What I'm about to tell you isn't going to be easy to hear. I need you all to stay with me just long enough for me to finish. Sarah went to town to try to make contact with the commissioner, but it didn't go as planned. It sounds like the solar storm was far worse than they predicted," Meredith said.

"How much worse?" someone asked.

Meredith's eyes shot to Sarah. "The nation has gone dark; it's suspected the effects have gone global."

There was a notable rumble among the group. Sarah could see they were already starting to panic.

"This can't be real; the nation is prepared for something like this!" someone yelled.

"It doesn't look like we were," Meredith said. "I know many of you have questions, and several of you have families waiting for you back home. I am not going to ask that any of you with families stay here with us. You can leave at any time. If you don't have family, we could use your help in—"

"In what?" someone asked. "What do you plan on

doing with the inmates? We can't take care of them forever."

"We are still working on putting together a plan. What I can tell you is that our compound now houses not only inmates, but a built-in workforce, weapons, and supplies. If you stay here, you will be safe. Once you leave, we cannot protect you. Those of you who are leaving can go now. You can take your firearms as well, but nothing else. We can't afford to lose the supplies."

Sarah watched in shock as twelve of the twenty guards headed for the gate. She knew many of them had families, but a few left without anyone waiting for them back home. It was easy to see the surprise in Meredith's eyes as well, but she quickly recovered to address the remaining eight guards. She drew a ragged breath.

"I don't know how we're going to do anything yet, but we are going to get a plan together and figure it out," Meredith said. "I appreciate anyone staying, and I hope we can work through this together."

"I don't know how long I can stay," one of the guards said. "Until then, what would you like us to do?"

"I'm going to break you up into a few different units. I think it will be safer if we stick together."

"That's a good idea, but what are we going to tell the inmates? We're going to have to give them something," Sarah said.

"Honestly, I don't know what to tell them," Meredith said. "I'm open to suggestions."

"I'm not really sure, either," Sarah replied. "I can tell

you one thing for sure, and that's the fact that I need a smoke."

Meredith chuckled and pulled out a pack from her shirt pocket. Sarah couldn't help but smile as she watched the woman open her pack of cigarettes and pull one out. She took it from her hand and put it to her mouth, thanking her boss as she did.

"I don't think we're going to be able to take care of the inmates for very long," the guard said. "Even if we ration out what supplies we do have, we have a month at best. What do we do when the food runs out?"

"We'll cross that bridge when we get there," Meredith replied. "For now, we take care of them the best we can."

Sarah sighed. "He's right. Even with the stock we have, we can't care for them very long."

"I'm open to any ideas."

The group went silent, half of them smoking, though Sarah was sure that hadn't been the case the day before. It didn't matter anymore. They were all realizing the same thing she had on the way home. The world around them had changed overnight, and they were reeling from it. The only chance that any of them had at survival now was working together. They had to devise a plan to preserve the maximum number of resources and lives. As an idea started to take shape in her mind, her heart raced. They could make it work, and if they did, she could leave to help her parents with a clear conscience.

13

"I think I have a plan," Sarah said.

The group quieted down, every head turning to look in her direction. Sarah was still working out the details in her mind. They were a low-security facility. Most of the inmates had committed non-violent crimes. Only a handful of the inmate population, roughly thirty, posed a true danger to society. Those were the men she would line up on the wall and execute before she considered setting them free. They were admitted killers and rapists, men with no remorse. The only reason they were at the prison was due to policy. The location was a hold-over for men being transported to their final locations.

"Are you going to share with the class?" Meredith asked.

"I'm still working it out, but the men we have here are not hardened criminals. They are tax evaders and petty thieves. What if we gave them the choice of going free or staying and working? This place is safer than anywhere else right now out there. We can condense the inmates we don't want to set loose into one block. The men who stay can work for their room and board," Sarah said.

"Let me get this straight. You want to set them free?" Alan asked.

Sarah nodded. "We already know this place will hold for a month tops with the numbers we have right now. That's eight guards trying to take care of hundreds of inmates. We won't be getting power back for months, a year even. This place is going to fall if we try to keep running it like a prison."

"She's right," Harden said.

"So, how do we do this?" someone asked.

Meredith didn't answer, instead turning to Sarah as if she were the one in charge. Her heart pounded when she realized everyone was looking to her for guidance. Not once had she considered running the operation, but now, it seemed to be the only path forward.

"I think we should look at the list of inmates we have," Sarah said. "Meredith, you should have a hard copy we can check out, right?"

"Yeah, I'll grab it from my office."

"Good. Alan, you can let John and Adam out and have them meet me in the courtyard. We're going to need a few extra pairs of hands no matter what we do, and the two of them can be helpful."

"I think you're right about that. Also, Barns and

Conners are both farm boys. They could be helpful, as well."

"Well, let them out, too. Bring them all to the courtyard, and we'll give them a heads-up as to what the plan is for now. Do any of you have any others who would be safe enough to help?" Sarah asked.

"I think there are a few in every block who could give us a hand and would be trustworthy," Meredith said. "Like you said, there aren't very many hardened criminals in here."

"Good. I think we should start by clearing out D block first. The less area we have to cover, the better. Bring me four inmates from each block who would be willing to give a hand and that you trust."

"They're inmates, for crying out loud," one guard said. "You're saying we should just trust these guys?"

"Yes, that's exactly what I'm saying. We're not going to be able to do this with only eight people, and I know there has to be a few from every block who are either getting ready to get out or are here on some garbage charges."

"What about the guard towers?"

"The two of you who came from the towers should go back and keep an eye out for anything."

As everyone separated to do the tasks she'd assigned, Sarah worked to calm her nerves. Her palms started to sweat when the doors to her block opened, and Adam stepped outside into the courtyard with John at his side. How was she going to explain to them what was going on? She watched them approach with her thoughts racing. Thankfully, John was his usual self despite the obviously grim circumstances. She wasn't surprised to find him smiling and laughing like they were set free every day.

"Dang, Fowler! I knew you were good, but this is damn impressive! What do we owe the special treatment to?" John asked.

"The world coming to an end, John."

His smile faltered. "Do what now?"

Sarah quickly explained to the pair what was happening and what her plan moving forward was. She told them they had a decision to make. They could work for the next twenty-four hours and then go free, or they could stay and have shelter, protection, and everything the compound had to offer. Before long, the other freed inmates would be coming out, and she'd have to repeat the conversation again. It was a task she could delegate to others but knowing Adam's decision was what she wanted most.

"I've got nowhere to be," John said. "If what you're saying is true, then this is the best place for us all. Now, will we be locked up the same as always?"

"We haven't gotten that far yet. I don't think that's going to be necessary, though," Sarah said.

"What about me? Am I getting locked back up?" Adam asked.

Her heart pounded as she shook her head. "I couldn't do that to you if I wanted to," Sarah said. "I've seen the emails firsthand. You're a free man, Adam. If you decide to stay and help us out, it will be as a free man and not an inmate. So, no. You won't be locked back up."

"Then I'm going to stay and help with whatever you need." Adam smiled. "Besides, Argentina is a long walk, and I don't think I've had that much exercise in years."

"I was hoping you'd say that, but it's going to be a lot of hard work to get this place set up to be sufficient enough for the other inmates here."

"I'm not worried about doing hard work. Plus, I have to say the scenery here is much better than what I'd find out there now."

"I'd say you're probably right. Who knows what people are doing out there."

"What about you, Sarah? I can only assume your parents are going to need you."

Sarah chuckled. "I don't know that they'll need much help to survive, but I am worried about them taking in the wrong type of people. They've always been too helpful. Once everything is taken care of here, I plan on leaving."

"Where did you say your parents lived?" Adam asked.

"Up north, in Maine. I figure a couple of days here to ensure the safety of the people here the best I can, then I'll be heading that way."

"Well, I've always wanted to see the northern states. I haven't been in any state up in that corner of the country."

She felt a flush jump to her cheeks, but before she

could reply, the doors to A block opened, and two inmates appeared. Giving a nod to John and Adam, she turned to the approaching inmates. By the time she'd repeated the conversation, Meredith was joining her in the courtyard, followed by two inmates carrying several long tables from the block's common room. Everything seemed to be progressing.

They worked for hours through the list of inmates. When it was nearing dusk, they had one hundred inmates who wanted to stay, and the rest had left the facility, leaving twenty-three high-risk inmates locked in D block. C block was now dedicated to the freed inmates staying at the compound. B block now housed all of the facility's food and resources. It would be guarded by two of the officers at all times. Just because they trusted the freed inmates didn't mean she wanted to risk anyone's getting wild ideas. The last block was where the guards were now sleeping.

While the arrangement wasn't ideal, it would work. As the inmates earned trust, they could do more and help protect the facility. Thankfully, the secluded location would keep them safer than other locations. The sun had started to go down, cooling the compound and the now-propped-open doors. Men mingled in the courtyard while several worked on cooking over an open fire. She was amazed by how peaceful everything was but knew it couldn't last forever.

Eventually, someone would come knocking at the door, and it would be up to the guards and inmates to work together to keep everyone safe. Sarah couldn't think about the compound's future, not when she had her own family to worry about. From the corner of her eye, she caught Adam watching her from where he was talking with John near the cooking tables. Her mind drifted back to his flirtatious words from earlier as she headed toward the men cooking dinner.

14

"What a day, huh?" John asked.

Sarah gave a low whistle. "You aren't kidding. So, how does it feel to be free?"

"A little strange, even weirder that I'm here of my own free will. Never thought I'd see the day when that happened," John said.

"I can't imagine," Sarah said.

Her eyes flickered to Adam, the blush jumping to her cheeks instantly. John, bless his heart, seemed to notice it and quickly made an excuse to disappear. She couldn't help but feel a little strange standing there with Adam despite knowing he was a free man. One who had been wrongfully imprisoned from the start. Yet she couldn't deny the racing in her heart as she fumbled for words. It was something she'd never expected to feel for anyone, let alone an inmate.

Did he really want to go with her to Maine? It wasn't

something she had the time to think about with everything happening. The day had been packed full of non-stop chaos. Their conversation earlier had been the familiar flirtatious one. Surely, he hadn't been serious in his offer to go north with her. Even thinking about the possibility made her stomach flutter. From what she knew about Adam, he had no problem with her taking charge of situations. He respected her as an independent individual, and she appreciated him for that.

The only way she could know for sure was by being direct with the man. Never in her life had she struggled with that, but around Adam, everything changed. She wasn't looking for someone to take control of things, but having someone on the trip to watch her back would be incredibly helpful. Plus, from his background, she knew he was smart and resourceful. He had taught a half dozen survival classes since starting his time at Glenwood.

"Adam, I have to know something," Sarah said.

"Okay. What do you want to know?"

"I've been wondering all day, and I need to know if you were serious about what you said earlier?"

Adam chuckled. "What do you mean?"

"Would you really consider going north with me to Maine? I mean, it's a pretty state and all, but it's a long way from Florida or Argentina."

"If I'm being completely honest with you, Sarah, you're the only reason I am still here."

Sarah could feel an instant rush of blood to her face. The blushing wasn't something she would ever get used to, and she still didn't quite understand her feelings for the man she had been in charge of for the last several years. None of it made sense, but maybe it made more sense now that he had been exonerated. After all, he wasn't the man who had been arrested and charged years before. Still, Adam had a way of making her feel something she hadn't felt in a very long time, and the idea that he wanted to come with her was exciting.

"Well, I've been thinking about it, and I'm planning on staying here until tomorrow night. I'm going to go north just after dark," Sarah said.

"Why are you waiting until nighttime?"

"I can use the cover of dark to make my way up the coast. I think it will be a lot safer, especially since I have no idea what it's like out there and how people are reacting."

"That's actually quite smart," Adam said. "You know, I'd love to accompany you north. I would understand completely if you don't want me to, but I think two people on the road like that would be safer than you doing it alone."

As Meredith blew a whistle from the guard tower platform, their conversation was cut short. She was grateful for the interruption. It gave her time to think about her reply. Of course, she wanted him to go. Sarah also wanted to make it clear that she didn't have time for a romantic relationship. Her only goal was to get to her parents' property and make sure they were safe. In all honesty, she was only waiting until the following night because she felt an obligation to Meredith. Once Sarah left, Meredith would be the only female at the compound.

The overwhelming urge to get to her parents was consuming her. They were smart but way too kind for the world they were now living in. Making their way over to stand by the others, Sarah watched as Meredith readied herself to speak. It was such a strange change from the atmosphere that had started the day. Everyone was happy, even cheerful, as they quietly gathered around. Had she not known it was a prison compound, it would have felt like a massive family reunion. She could see the men respected Meredith, and that comforted her some.

"Everyone, I'd just like to say a few words. I can't tell you how proud I am of each and every one of you. What we accomplished today and what we are going to do moving forward is really going to be something for the history books. I know many of you are anxious to get back to the festivities. Let's keep in mind there is a curfew at ten. Tomorrow we'll start preparing to grow crops, and hopefully when this is all over, and the lights come back on, we'll be just as happy as we are right now. Have a great night, everyone."

As Meredith started to come back down, Adam gave her a smile and turned to talk with John. With a plan in place, Sarah had to tell Meredith what she was going to do. She wanted to give her friend as much notice as possible. On top of that, Sarah had to tell Meredith that

Adam was going to come with her. It wasn't something she was looking forward to explaining.

"I would have never imagined that we could accomplish all of this in such a short time frame," Meredith said. "It's going much better than I ever thought it could."

"It is, but I knew it could be done. Listen, we need to talk."

Meredith sighed. "I knew this was going to come. I've been waiting for you to approach me and tell me you're leaving. When do you plan on heading out?"

"Tomorrow night. It's going to be a long journey up the coast, and the longer I'm here, the more I'm starting to worry about my parents. I wish there was a way to get them a message, but that's no longer possible. I need to make sure they're okay."

"Well, no one here can fault you on that. I wish I could get them that message. You've been so much help to me here, and I can't thank you enough for helping me get this all up and going."

"Just doing my job."

Meredith chuckled. "I'm pretty sure this qualifies for going above and beyond. All I can say is thank you for staying a few extra days and helping with this. I'm grateful you made that choice."

"They deserve a chance to survive as much as anyone else," Sarah said. "Besides, if we didn't do it, who would?"

"No one else would have done what we've done. That was made evident by the number of people who left the moment they could."

"Exactly," Sarah said. "There's something else I need to tell you."

"What is it, Sarah?"

"I haven't been sure how to tell you, so I'll just come right out with it. When I leave tomorrow night, I'm going to be taking Adam with me."

Meredith gave her a quizzical look but didn't ask any more questions as a group of men approached and started asking her a few questions. Sarah took the time to slip away from the woman. If she was going to leave and now have a second person with her on foot, they had to be extremely careful and prepared. There was a map of the surrounding area in her office and a compass in her car. Her father had given it to her the year before.

Thanks to her generally cluttered life, it hadn't made it out of the glove box. As long as they kept heading north and stayed along the coast, they could make it there in good time. Changing directions, she headed for the staff parking lot to scour her car for anything they might be able to use. Sarah was excited about hitting the road before but now, knowing she'd have Adam with her, she couldn't wait to leave.

Shaking her head, Sarah reminded herself that she needed to keep her head in the game. As she left the compound and reached her car, she popped open the trunk with the key but only after trying the remote-control button first out of habit. When she remembered the gear still loaded for the gym in the back, Sarah knew it was going to be okay.

15

The next morning, she was packing the bag she'd found in her car along with the bookbag from the storage room. With Meredith's blessing, she had taken enough food and two water purifiers from their stock supply. It wasn't a favor Sarah would soon forget. Once her parents were safe and settled, she promised Meredith she'd be back to check in on her. She was going to meet Adam after the sun went down around eight at the front gate. Others had left during the day, and they'd been able to watch them for miles on the flat terrain.

She wanted the cover of darkness as they moved. By day, they could find shelter along the coast. Avoiding the cities wasn't her only reason for taking the coast to Maine. They could take shelter at dozens of restaurants, bars, and boat houses that would now be abandoned. Word had quickly spread through the compound about Adam and Sarah's pending departure. Later that morn-

THE LAST HOMESTEAD

ing, Meredith announced the departure of the pair, along with three more inmates and Alan. With each new person who left the prison compound, Sarah knew Meredith was torn.

On the one hand, fewer mouths to feed would make the supplies go further, but it also meant fewer hands working to prepare themselves. Taking care of thirty convicts in cells was no small task on its own. Throwing in the fact that they had no power and Sarah was forced to wonder how long it would be before executions were the only humane option. Once again, she was thankful the decision didn't rest on her shoulders. The day passed without incident until Sarah found herself waiting at the front gate for her travel partner.

Alan emerged and smiled at her with his backpack ready for the trek ahead. He was heading ten miles south to his home and wife. Sarah wished she could go with him, but she had her own family to worry about. It was bittersweet not knowing if they would ever see each other again. Sarah tried to keep her spirits hopeful that they would find each other again when the world went back to normal. She just didn't know if that day would ever come. Was it possible the world that surrounded them was a new reality?

"Are you all set to make the trip up north?" Alan asked.

"I think so, but I have no idea what I'm going to run into along the way. God only knows what the world is like out there, and if movies are any indication of how the world reacts to these situations, we're in for some rough days."

"Yeah, but I'm hoping movies are just what they are—visual stories."

Sarah chuckled. "Well, I'm with you on that thought, but I'm not optimistic about it."

"Sadly, neither am I. I have to ask if you think taking Adam with you is a good idea. I know he's been found innocent, but what do you really know about the man?"

"He was wrongfully convicted. The corrupt system put him here to either cover up for someone else or to cover their own mistakes. Either way, he deserves to have a chance out there."

"Yeah, but that doesn't mean he's a good guy," Alan replied. "That just means he didn't do what they said he did. You only know him from in here, and you know how people can just pretend to be something they're not, so it looks good for their parole."

"I understand your position, Alan. He's worth taking a chance on, and I've researched his case a lot. His interviews and his attitude in here—even with being wrongfully convicted, he was a model inmate."

"Well, I've never been one to question your intentions, and I'm not going to start now. I just want to make sure that you're making the right choice. I worry about you, Sarah. If I didn't ask if you were sure, Becky would have my ass in a sling."

Sarah chuckled. "She's probably going to anyway."

"You're probably right."

"Still, I trust my instincts. They've never steered me wrong before."

"I trust your instincts, too."

Alan pulled her into his arms and gave her a loving bear hug. When he pulled away, he unlocked the gate before handing her his keys. It broke her heart to watch him go as she locked the gate behind him. He gave one final wave to her and Meredith as she approached. Seeing her friend disappear down the road was difficult, but she knew it was coming. The next part was going to be just as difficult. The compound and the friendships she'd made over the years wouldn't be easy to forget.

Nor did she want to, they had become her second family, but her first one needed her more. Everything would be okay as long as Meredith was running things. She refused to believe the country wouldn't quickly rebound from what was happening. The middle-aged woman smiled at her with tears glistening in her eyes. If she'd been hoping for a quick and emotionless goodbye, Sarah was going to be disappointed. Meredith had been a surrogate mother to her while her own was hundreds of miles away.

"I can't believe you're really going. I don't know what I'm going to do without you," Meredith said.

"John is a great man; he's going to help you run things, and he's got a great rapport with the inmates," Sarah said.

"He's not you, and you're taking the only innocent man here with you, don't think that one slipped by me."

Sarah blushed and quickly looked away from the captain. Sarah didn't know what to say to the woman when she didn't know what was going on herself with Adam. All she knew was that he'd be an asset to her on the road. Once she got to Maine, it would be his decision if he wanted to stay or not. She shook her head and turned her attention back to Meredith, who was still waiting on an answer from her. There was no one coming to save her from the awkward conversation now.

"I know you're worried, but you should know we're only friends," Sarah said. "There's nothing going on between the two of us."

Meredith chuckled. "I didn't ask." Meredith chuckled.

"I've really gotten to know him over the years after studying his case and keeping track of it. He's a good egg, and I only want him to have the opportunity to prove it."

"Well, I, for one, have never questioned your judgment. I just want you to make sure you're safe out there."

"I promise I'm going to be as safe as I can. As soon as I get up to my parents' place, I'll find a way to send word back to you that I made it safe," Sarah said. "Are you sure you're going to be okay?"

"Honestly, I have no other place to be, and these guys need my help. Plus, I have to be the one to keep the public safe. Just because these men haven't done anything hardcore doesn't mean that they don't deserve to be here."

"I know if there is anyone who can do that, it's going to be you, but I'm still going to worry about you."

"I'll be fine. This has been my life for a long time. I never saw myself doing anything else."

"Well, you take care of yourself, Meredith. Look after your men and yourself."

"I planned on it. You just make sure you're safe, too. I think it's going to be rough out there."

"It will be, but I'll manage."

"I know you will," Meredith said. "Thank you, Sarah. You've been an immense help to me and this place."

"You're welcome. I promise I'll be fine."

When Meredith pulled Sarah into her arms, she had no idea how to hold back the tears. It was only when she saw Adam approaching that she managed to pull herself out of the heartbreak. She had no idea if she would ever see her friend again, but she was excited to get on the road. Wiping away the tears, she smiled once more at her friend as Adam stopped next to the pair. In the same manner Alan had done moments before, Sarah unlocked the gate before handing her key over to Meredith.

"Take good care of her," Meredith said.

Adam gave her a nod, a silent promise that he would as they set off down the road. Her heart pounded in the silence that fell around them. Sarah was happy they were finally on the road and heading for her parents' homestead, but the looming dread had returned. The sooner she got to Maine, the better she would feel. They needed her now more than ever. She quickened her pace. They had a long road ahead of them.

16

They moved silently. It was strange to be out on the road at night with nothing else in sight. In the pack, they had a dozen candles and MREs, but she didn't want to use them until it was absolutely necessary. As long as the moon stayed above them without clouds, they could see the road in front of them. It would take them as far as town. They could cross through the small city without problems and hopefully unnoticed under the cover of night. Once the road split, it was only a few miles to the coast where they could start moving north.

She knew most of the terrain well. With only the compass to guide them, they needed to be careful with their supplies. If they got off track, they could be stranded, and with a limited amount of food, it could get dangerous. They would catch their dinner off the coast for as long as possible when the tide and weather permitted. They didn't stop or speak until she could see the outline of the village in the moonlight ahead of them. Given their proximity to the prison, she knew they should be prepared for the worst.

Hopefully, the influx of prisoners into the area hadn't disrupted their lives too much. Everyone they released was low risk, but that didn't mean much, given the circumstances. People could change on a dime. It was too much to risk going down the main road. The map she'd taken from the crow's nest showed her a small ravine that ran along the edge of the community. It would cover their tracks and keep them away from the main population. Suddenly, a figure emerged near the edge of the town. Sarah grabbed Adam and pulled him into the trees and brush along the road before they were spotted.

"What is it, Sarah? What do you see?" Adam asked.

"The man has a shotgun."

"You can tell that from this distance? Where?"

"It's propped up against his shoulder. I can see the form in the shadow. From what I can see, it's definitely a shotgun, and I'd rather not find out what model it is."

"What are we going to do now? Is there another way to go around, or would it be better to just wait him out?"

Sarah sighed as she thought about what to do next. While she had planned on running into people with weapons, she had no idea what kind of man was ahead of them. She quickly glanced around the area between them and the man with the gun. Trying to find any way to move around him without being noticed. When she saw that the ravine beside them seemed to move in the direction of the town, she knew they needed to take the low road.

"I think our best shot of moving around unnoticed is to head down that ravine. We'll cross through that way," Sarah said.

"I barely even noticed that thing in the dark," Adam said. "Say, how do you know all this stuff?"

Sarah chuckled quietly. "Well, my parents taught me a bunch of things while I was growing up. They wanted me to be prepared for anything."

"So, they taught you how to spot a gun in the dead of night, along with what directions to take?"

"They taught me a lot of different things. I could live off the land for months without ever needing anyone else."

"They sound nice, but I think you must have had those doomsday-prepper kind of parents."

"That's putting it lightly, but it's coming in handy now."

"I can attest to that." Adam chuckled. "Should we go now?"

"No, I'll tell you when to move."

When the guard was no longer visible, Sarah moved quietly through the brush to where the map showed the small stream of water moving beyond the town. She climbed down despite the darkness shrouding them, thanks to the trees. It was too much of a risk to use their candles to light the way. All she could do was listen for the water beneath her waterproof boots. Thankfully, they had an extra pair of boots in the storeroom, so she knew Adam's feet were staying dry as well.

They were making good time considering their pace. They followed the water to where it crossed beneath a fork in the road. It took them a little under an hour to make the five-mile trek to the fork. Climbing back out of the water, she stomped her feet on the rocks before heading down the road that would take them to the ocean. She could hear it in the distance, something that normally wouldn't happen. Without the constant buzz of mankind's evolution over the land, there was so much more to hear.

She couldn't wait to reach the water, but Adam was starting to fall behind. It was understandable after ten years of incarceration. No matter how much exercise you got, fresh air and the constantly changing terrain of Mother Nature were challenging on an inmate's body. Plus, she was accustomed to being active all night. It had to be yet another shock to Adam's system. They needed to reach the water and get a few miles up the coast before the sun came up. Still, Sarah slowed her pace until Adam was at her side again. He breathlessly smiled at her and shook his head in dismay.

"So, how are you holding up so far?" Sarah asked.

"It's intense, but I'm doing okay. I haven't had to move around like this in quite a while, but I'll manage."

"We only have a few more hours of night left. We're going to have to move quickly if we want to be across state lines when the sun comes up again."

"Is that what you're thinking we need to do?" Adam asked. "Cross over before the day starts?"

"For sure. If we want to get through this in one piece and stay out of danger, we need to move at a pretty high pace. It's not the best plan, I know, but it's the only way to get through all the people who will be out and about during the day."

"Well, you lead the way. Whatever pace you want us to keep, I'll keep up with you."

"Are you sure you're going to be able to handle that kind of exertion?" Sarah chuckled.

Adam laughed. "Are you trying to bet me that I can't keep up with you?"

"Maybe not a bet, but it's definitely going to be a challenge. This isn't the terrain you've been accustomed to in prison."

"That's true, but it's not like I haven't kept myself in some kind of shape while I was there."

"You're hour of rec time is making you feel pretty confident."

"I bet I'll be able to keep up with you. Just lead the way."

"You said I was making challenges. Look who's laying down the bets now."

Adam winked at her. "Don't go worrying about me. I won't fall too far back. Besides, there's nothing more I want than to follow you."

Sarah laughed as she picked up her pace. If he wanted to play that game, she was happy to do so. Knowing her parents were waiting for them was a huge motivator. They moved quickly in the direction of the beach until she felt the sand beneath her boots and saw the waves moving beneath the moonlight. It was a huge relief, but they still had a ways to go. Moving along the coast had its advantages. Their obstacles would be limited, but the sand still took some time to adjust to walking on.

Adam was still breathing heavily behind her, but to his credit, his pace hadn't slowed. It wasn't that she was trying to break him, but she had to start conditioning him for the long path ahead. Every day they'd need to push themselves a little harder if they were going to make it to Maine in good time. The minutes turned into hours as the sun started to peek above the water. As soon as the sky started to change, a lifeguard station came into view, and Sarah headed in its direction.

As she'd suspected, there was no one in sight. The door was unlocked, and the shades had all been drawn. If it hadn't been for her parents, it would make a perfectly secluded spot to set up shop for the months ahead. As it was, it would give them shelter for the day while they slept. When they finally collapsed on the floor, she couldn't believe just how exhausted she was. They had to talk about the next leg of the journey, but she was too tired to think. Watching Adam lock the door before lying back down on the floor, Sarah closed her eyes.

Everything else could wait. At that moment, they both needed sleep.

17

Six days later, they were both exhausted, but they had made great time. A trip that should have taken almost two weeks was already halfway over. As they walked beneath the sign indicating they'd reached Virginia Beach, Sarah grinned at Adam. With each passing day, she'd become more anxious about getting to her parents. They needed her there to keep them safe. The trip had been almost entirely void of other people. The pair had come across the occasional fisher or family trying to escape the new reality, but otherwise, it had been quiet.

As soon as they reached Virginia, Sarah knew it would be different. It was far too crowded in the surrounding cities for it not to spill out onto the beaches. A detour would take them days out of the way, and that was time she wasn't willing to lose. They'd decided as a team to take the most direct route. Moving along the coast, Sarah wondered if they'd made the wrong decision as campfires speckled the beach ahead of them.

After the last near week on the road with Adam, the pair no longer needed to use words to communicate their path. Sarah jerked her head in the direction of the marsh that separated the beach from the towering hotels that lined it. It felt like years since she'd seen the beach. It no longer mattered that the marshes were protected. Nature would soon reclaim far more than it had in the decades before, thanks to the solar storm.

It was still hard to believe, even after seeing it with her own eyes, that so much had changed. Cities that had once been thriving metropolises had been thrown into chaos. They could hear people screaming and gunshots from miles away. Sarah wanted to help them, but there was nothing she could do. They needed an army to rescue them, not two lone travelers. As they inched closer to the campfires, Sarah heard the group near the end talking amongst themselves. There were three of them.

"Did you find anything good out there?" the first man asked.

"Shit, there's nothing out there that hasn't been looted already. I think we might have to move on to another spot. Either that or try to take over one of these larger houses where people are holing up."

"Now, you know we can't go doing that. There's strength in numbers that we just don't have."

"Yeah, but I don't know what we're going to do after

our supplies run out."

"We'll figure it out when the time comes. For now, we'll just keep looking for anything to get us by. What about you?"

The first man seemed to be the leader of the group. He was a large man and had a thick accent. Sarah couldn't be sure of anything at that point, but her instinct was telling her that the men were bad news. Just the fact that they had mentioned taking control of anything had her wondering what type of men they were. While her heart was already pounding with anticipation, she quietly waited to hear the rest of the conversation.

"Well, I went down to the shop, and there were a couple of girls in there."

"Oh yeah?" the man grunted. "You talking about that shop around the corner?"

"The one and the same, and there were two sweet things just waiting for a few men like us. Plus, they were pretty easy on the eyes, too. I imagine it would be easy to grab the pair of them and have our way with them."

"How much fight do you think they'd put up?"

"Oh, they would probably struggle a bit, but isn't that half the fun of it? I don't think it would be hard to get what we wanted out of them."

"Well, damn, boy. What in the hell are we waiting for?"

Adam's gaze fell on Sarah. She knew they couldn't sit back and do nothing while the men raped two innocent girls. As the trio rose and stumbled past them, too drunk to notice they were there, they leaped into action. Between both of their skills, it was easy to bring the trio down, but neither had anticipated the noise it would cause. Minutes after the three men were lying in the marsh unconscious, Sarah saw the glow of an approaching mob from farther down the beach. They had to move and fast if they were going to get away.

Grabbing Adam's hand without thinking, she darted for the main strip, once bustling with happy vacationers. Now, those who remained were either desperate to leave or desperate not to be found. The shop had an attached garage that sloped down onto a lower level. The large garage door was already standing open. She could hear someone below them making a good bit of noise. In a split second, she made the decision to head down.

It didn't take long for them to find the two girls the men had been talking about. They couldn't have been older than eighteen, but the instant they saw the pair racing toward them, the girls had guns drawn. She skidded to a stop and lifted her hands over her head. Adam, thankfully, did the same. They didn't have much time before the mob of people found their friends beat to a pulp and started to give chase. If any of them were going to make it out of there alive, they needed to work together, but more so, they needed to get moving right away.

"Look, I don't mean to startle you, and we certainly don't mean any harm, but we need to find a way out of here or someplace to lay low for a little bit," Sarah said.

"What do you mean?"

"There's a small mob coming for you right now."

"Why in the hell are they coming for us, and why should we help you?" the girl asked. "We don't have the slightest idea as to who you are."

"We saw a few men at the edge of town talking to one another, and they said they were going to come to grab you. My friend and I took them down, but now there's a mob looking for us, and I'm sure once the others get moving again, they'll come back for both of you."

"Why would you help us?"

"Just because the world has gone to shit doesn't mean that all of humanity has. There are still good people out here, but that doesn't mean they all are," Sarah said.

"I don't know what to do. We didn't ask for you to help us. Maybe they'll just keep moving if they know someone was looking out for us."

"You can take that chance, and it's up to you, but right now, we have to get going. You can come with us, but if you do, we need to get going right now."

The first girl looked at the second with a growing concern in her eyes. "Go grab the others and tell them we're leaving."

"What others?" Sarah asked, confused.

Her stomach rolled with anticipation as one of the girls disappeared into the belly of the dark garage. Suddenly, Sarah heard something she hadn't in years. At least not since she had been a little girl on her parents' homestead. The noise was still a familiar one to her as a horse nickered from the darkness seconds before emerging at the end of the lead line. The two young girls were not without an escape. The opposite seemed to be true. As a matter of fact, they were helping Adam and Sarah escape from the mob.

"These are Ginger, George, Grasshopper, and Greg... our parents were really into *G*s," one of the girls said with a blush.

Sarah chuckled. "What about you two? Do you have names that start with *G*s as well?"

"Nope, I'm Rose, and that's Bella," the older one said.

"What about your parents?" Adam asked.

Bella cringed, but it was Rose who continued to speak as she handed the reins for one of the horses to Sarah and the other to Adam. The girls mounted up, and Sarah followed suit. Only Adam appeared uncomfortably unaware of what he was supposed to do to get onto the steed's back.

"Dad died last year, and Mom's on a cruise with her new boyfriend. We were down here for a show. We've got a farm in New Jersey," Rose said.

"We're headed to Maine," Adam said. He'd finally managed to climb onto the horse's back.

"Then I suggest we get out of here and fast unless we all want to make new friends with that mob you said is coming," Bella said.

The others nodded in agreement. There would be time to get to know each other later. At that moment, they needed to get out of town.

18

It was impossible to move quietly through the streets with the horses. Their shoed hooves clattered against the blacktop as the foursome raced down the street. Sarah's history with horses wasn't deep or long, but she knew enough to get by. Her parents had two horses when she was a child, but after they passed of old age on the property, they'd decided not to get more. By that time, Sarah was just starting high school, and her world was her friends and education. Still, it gave her enough insight to know what she was doing for the most part.

Glancing behind her, she saw that Adam was struggling to stay in the saddle as his horse trotted along with the others. She couldn't help but chuckle a little to herself. The two young women were incredibly resilient. Without slowing, they continued down the main drag as the sound of the mob behind them started to fall into the distance. They couldn't stop until they were as far away from the danger as they could safely get with the horses. She had no idea how riding would change their trajectory. While the animals could cut their travel time in half, it also meant more mouths to feed.

They couldn't catch fish and feed them to the animals, and they'd need a fresh water source as well. While the sisters seemed to be prepared for their journey, they were obviously still frightened, and Sarah could understand why. She wondered what all the girls knew about what was going on as they raced across the bridge that would take them to Ocean City in Maryland. As soon as the horses crossed onto the sand, Sarah understood they'd be just fine staying along the coastal water.

When they'd put a good ten miles between themselves and the popular beach community, they finally slowed to a walk to give the horses a break. Seeing her opportunity to find out more about their new companions, Sarah stretched out and looked back at Rose and Bella, who were in the middle between Adam and herself.

"So, how long have you all been traveling, Bella?" Sarah asked.

"We've been moving since everything went dark. We hadn't been at the shop long, but we knew we had to keep going."

"What about when this all started? Where were you when the solar storm passed through?"

"We were all staying at a bed and breakfast that had a

stable. Before the first night was through, it got overrun by people. It's been a real mess from the start," Bella said.

"We barely even got out of there," Rose said. "We grabbed the horses and tack, and we didn't bother to look back. As soon as people knew there wouldn't be anyone to stop them, the chaos started."

"I knew it would get pretty bad, but I had no idea people would lose their minds that fast. I figured we would still have some time to travel before chaos completely erupted," Sarah said. "I'm glad you made it out of there."

"You mentioned something about a solar storm," Rose said. "I remember seeing something about that, or maybe I overheard someone talking about it. Is that what started all of the power outages in the area?"

"From what I understand, the solar storm passed through and caused everything to go into darkness. We've been on the road for less than a week, but it's something that seems to have affected everything."

"So, we're not the only ones going through the power outage? Is it something that is localized to the East Coast?"

Sarah's eyes darted to Adam. She knew she had to tell the girls the world was in turmoil. Their mother, depending on where she was, might never make it back home to them. Her heart lurched for the young pair. Even once they reached the girls' home, could Sarah leave them alone with a clear conscience? They were both so young. She couldn't think about it at that moment. They had a right to know what was happening in the world around them. Sarah cleared her throat and quickly told the sisters everything they knew about the solar storm and the disaster that had followed it.

When she was finally finished, they rode for some time in silence. Sarah knew the girls were struggling to process everything she'd just told them. It had been hard for her to hear for the first time and to tell others. The reality of their situation, though, was dire. Sarah had to make sure the girls were prepared for whatever they might face when they reached their mother's property.

If bandits and roving gangs hadn't already ransacked it, Sarah knew they'd come eventually. The closer the nation got to winter, the more desperate people would become. As long as they were together, they had some level of safety, but the girls were young and attractive. The sleazebags would be crawling out of the woodwork now. Without knowing what the pair's plans were once, they reached New Jersey.

"Do you have any more family out at your mom's place, or is your family all here?" Sarah asked.

"There isn't any more family, but the housekeeper is still there. Should be at least," Rose said.

"Look, I can't promise what we find there is going to be good. I need you to be prepared for whatever you see. If the mobs were that bad back that way, then you know they're going to be like that everywhere."

"What do you mean?" Bella asked. "It's not like there's a lot there for people to take."

"Yeah, but people could have taken over the property itself. It's hard telling what people are looking for, but I'm sure that having a safe and warm place to stay is at the top of the list. There's just no telling what we're going to find there."

"If that's the case, then we'll fight to take it back. That's our property," Bella said.

While Sarah was happy to see such determination in the young woman, there was no telling what they would actually run into once they got them back home. The world was fighting amongst itself, and there were evil people running free throughout the country. Still, she could understand the urge to want to fight for what was rightfully hers. After all, it was one of the reasons she was heading back home to check on her parents. Part of her wanted to fight with Rose and Bella if the need arose, but the fact of the matter was that some things might be better left alone, and Bella needed to understand that.

"I just want you to understand that something like that might not be possible. If they have more people than we do or if we are outgunned, it might be better to just leave them be," Sarah said. "Still, we just don't have any idea what we're going to find when we get—"

"It doesn't matter what we find or who they have," Bella snapped. "We're not going to let our home fall into criminal's hands."

The group fell silent as they rode. Sarah wasn't going to press the issue anymore. It was obvious the conversation had upset Bella. While she didn't want to scare the young girls, she also wanted them to be prepared for the worst. Still, it was a lot to process all at once. Plus, there was no question in her mind that the girls were exhausted. It was no surprise, given how frightened they had to be in the week since the power went out. Sarah couldn't imagine being their age, alone in a city they didn't know when the entire world was going to shit.

Sarah silently made a promise to herself that she wouldn't let anything happen to the pair. They needed someone to look out for them, and she was happy to take on the responsibility. They had a two-day ride before they reached the girls' homestead if they moved quickly. At that time, Sarah had to convince them they were safer if they all stayed together. At the very least, she and Adam would need to stay with them at their mother's property long enough to make sure it was secure.

As her list of dependents grew, she prayed her parents were still safe and alive. Every detour they took pulled her farther away from getting to Harmony Homestead, where she was raised. Her conscience wouldn't let her turn her back on someone who needed them. All she could do was trust that her parents were capable of defending themselves for a little while longer. They would understand why it took her so long to get to them. The couple had raised Sarah with a strong moral compass. When someone needed her help, she would always answer the call.

19

The rest of the trip went without incident. She couldn't believe how amazing the two sisters truly were. Between the four of them, they managed to stay away from any roving groups of people. Keeping with the schedule they already had, the group moved primarily at night. To her surprise, the girls were incredibly well prepared to care for the horses but not themselves. They had taken great care before leaving the stable with the animals to ensure they had enough feed to last the entirety of the journey.

Yet they had almost nothing to keep themselves alive. Sarah was thrilled they had crossed paths and were now working together. The girls ate like they hadn't seen food in weeks each time she prepared a meal for the group. With their limited cooking abilities, Sarah tasked them with teaching Adam about the horses and catching their meals. It had been a while since their main dish was anything but seafood, yet all of their spirits remained high as the girls' homestead finally came into view.

Situated five miles from the coast, the seven-acre plot of land was nothing like Sarah had expected. From what she knew about the girls, their mother had worked two jobs to provide for them. She'd expected the home of a single mom for the most part, but the stable alone had to hover in the six-figure range alone. The house was equally as impressive. From where they were hidden in the forest across the street, they could see that the place looked untouched by looters and squatters, but Sarah wanted to approach with caution, nonetheless.

Bella started to move onto the road right away, but Sarah held her back and shook her head. She knew the girls were excited to finally be home. She was anxious to finally have a safe place to sleep for the night, too, but her primary focus was keeping everyone alive. She couldn't ensure their safety until she knew what was within the homestead first.

"We can't go in there just yet," Sarah said.

"Why not?" Bella asked. "It's not like there's anyone in there. You can see from here that it hasn't been overrun with people."

"Yeah, but we need to be careful and make sure—"

Before she could finish her sentence, Sarah noticed movement inside the house. It was faint, but it was easy to recognize the motion through the window. Without warning, the front door opened, and a woman stepped out onto the porch. While she had no idea who the woman was, Bella and Rose both had looks of recognition on their faces.

"I take it that's your housekeeper," Sarah said.

"Yeah, her name is Harriette, and she's been with us for a while now," Bella said. "I told you there was nothing to worry about. It looks like she's the only one here."

"It's okay," Rose said. "Harriette wouldn't do anything to put us in danger."

"She might not, but there could be other men inside who are in control. We have to be safe about this. I don't want anything to happen to you or anyone else. If they are holding her hostage, it wouldn't be hard to send her outside to trick people into coming in."

Rose smiled. "Thank you, but we have our own way of making sure things are okay. Bella, why don't you give her the signal."

"What do you mean?" Sarah asked. "What kind of signal?"

Bella smiled as they all turned their attention to the young woman. She stuck both her pinkies into her mouth and gave a low whistle that near perfectly mimicked a bird's call. Instantly, the woman on the porch froze. She had been sweeping dust off the front porch, but now she was stiff as the fencing boards running the length of the property. Her eyes searched around frantically for a split second before she dropped the broom in her hands and quickly whistled in a similar manner.

"That means it's all clear," Bella quickly said.

Before Sarah could stop her a second time, Bella raced out of the forest in the direction of the driveway. Instantly, the woman on the porch raced down the steps in Bella's direction. The horses beneath them started to prance with anticipation, and Sarah knew they couldn't hold them back any longer. Thankfully, the girls had taught her and Adam more about the animals in the last few days than either had ever known before. In one fluid movement, Bella was off her horse and racing to the woman's arms before the others even made it through the arches over the entrance.

As soon as Harriette realized there were other people with the two girls, she positioned herself between the strangers and the girls. Sarah couldn't help but feel overjoyed seeing how much the woman obviously cared for the pair. Rose quickly explained to Harriette that the two were friends of theirs, but Harriette didn't budge. Her cold gaze was leveled at Adam to the point that Sarah could feel the chill from where she sat on her mount several feet away.

"I'm going to have to ask you to step back," Harriette said. "I know that man there, and he's not welcome here. He's a murderer. It was all over the news, and I never forget a face."

"I was proven innocent," Adam said. "I wouldn't be here if they thought I was guilty."

"I haven't heard anything about that. I know they were looking into it, but there wasn't anything said before the power went out, and I'm not going to take any chances."

Sarah hadn't thought about the fact that Adam was a well-known face in the news. It had been such a high-profile case because of the unborn child that had been killed. She knew they would run into trouble along the way, but it never crossed her mind that someone would recognize him and cause a problem. Sarah knew he was innocent. She had seen the reports and was in direct contact with the prosecutor for the entire case, but the people in the world who had only watched the news hadn't been told yet. The report was supposed to go public a few days after the power went out.

"Look, everything he has said is the truth," Sarah said. "Not only is he telling the truth, but I can prove everything he is saying."

Sarah started to get down off her horse, but before she could, Harriette motioned for her to stop. Her heart started racing as she thought about the wrong that Adam had already gone through in his life. It was her turn to stand up for the man as she watched Harriette slowly close the distance between them.

"You just stop it right there. I know his face, but I don't know you, and I don't trust either one of you at this point," Harriette said. "Just don't move, and you won't have to worry about what will happen next."

"It's okay, Harriette," Bella said. "Take it from me that they are both friendly and mean us no harm. They helped us get here. So, please, just listen to what she has to say."

Climbing down off her horse, Sarah carefully took off her bookbag and unzipped the outside pocket. She had stuffed the documents in her bag before she'd left the prison. Grabbing the papers proving his innocence had been an afterthought she'd nearly forgotten while leaving her crow's nest for the last time. Now, as she handed the papers over to Harriette and explained who she was in relation to Adam, Sarah was relieved that she'd grabbed them. As Harriette read the decree from the judge, Sarah could see the tension easing from her shoulders.

Sarah stole a quick glance at Adam, still situated on his horse. He caught her looking and smiled at her, a silent nod in appreciation for what she'd done. Her heart raced as she thought of their first few nights together on the road when they'd been alone. The tender embers of something more had started to burn between them, but after finding the sisters, the only time they'd had alone was a stolen second on horseback. The romance she could see blossoming between them had once again been put on hold. Harriette folded the papers again and handed them to Sarah, but her eyes were on Adam.

"For ten years, you were locked up and innocent?" Harriette asked, shaking her head at the injustice.

Adam nodded. "Sarah here pushed for the truth. She's the reason I'm free."

Sarah blushed and shook her head. "Innocent is innocent. I would have done it for anyone."

She hated being the center of a conversation. Her role in his release had all been behind closed doors. Sarah had no idea Adam knew just how far she'd gone to secure his release. In her mind, it was all part of the job. An innocent man had no place in her prison. Not that it mattered now, the prison was no more.

20

"They saved our lives, too," Rose added. "Some creeps were fixing to have their way with us when these two showed up. They beat them to a pulp, then we helped them get out of there."

Harriette seemed impressed by what the girls were telling her. As quickly as she'd been to welcome the girls into her arms, she soon welcomed the newcomers, too. It didn't take long before the group was headed in the direction of the stable, and they got to learn more about the property and the protective woman. Harriette had worked for the previous owners of the homestead, Rose and Bella's grandfather.

When he had passed and his daughter inherited the property, she pleaded with Harriette to stay on. The woman was like a grandmother to the girls and had taken care of the farm any time the trio left. Walking into the stable made Sarah long for her own homestead and her parents. She was still grateful they had met the woman when they did. Even if they'd only gained a few extra days by using the horses, anything was better than being days behind. Now that the animals and girls were safely back home, she was ready to push forward on their journey.

First, they needed to sleep while they had the opportunity. Harriette insisted the group meet her on the back patio as soon as the animals were tended to. An hour after they first saw the property, they walked toward the house to where Harriette was waiting for them on a huge screened-in back porch. It was the kind of place you never wanted to leave. Sarah was comforted knowing the girls would be safe and cared for. Her stomach growled when they walked onto the porch, and she caught a whiff of something being cooked on the closed grill.

"Something really smells good," Sarah said.

"Yeah, I've got a duck and potatoes cooking for dinner. There's plenty enough for everyone," Harriette said. "If you've done what the girls said you did, then you're more than welcome to stay and have something to eat."

"Well, I, for one, am not going to turn down a good home-cooked meal," Adam said. "Thanks for the invitation. It smells amazing."

"The girls say you're trustworthy and helped keep those men away from them. It's the least I can do to thank you for saving them. Where are you two heading, anyway?"

"We've got family up in Maine we're trying to get to," Sarah said. "My parents have a nice homestead up there, and since this all started, I've been worried about them. So, I'd like to make sure they're okay first, but ultimately, I just want to help them out when we get there."

"Sounds like the two of you have a long road ahead of you. It's not going to be easy getting that far with no cars to carry you."

"That's one of the things I was going to talk to you about, Harriette. How many horses do you have?"

"Now that Bella and Rose have come back with the four they had, we have six total," Harriette said.

"Though, I think we're going to be back down to four soon," Bella said.

"What do you mean?" Sarah asked.

"I just figured that after all the help you've been for us, it would be all right if two of them left when you did. You're going to need them if you want to get to Maine faster than walking."

Sarah's gaze darted to Rose and Harriette. It was not something she'd expected, nor was it something they had discussed. The last thing she wanted was to take resources away from the homesteaders. If they'd had more than six, she would have tried to come up with some sort of trade, but taking two could put them in danger later. While the horses were incredibly valuable, they might need them to trade or flee if trouble came knocking. She quickly shook her head, ready to argue with the girl over the offer, but before she could, Harriette quickly excused the trio for a quick family discussion. Sarah turned to Adam, totally blown away as she shook her head.

"We can't take them, right?" Adam whispered.

"No way, they need them, or at least they might. I don't know how prepared they are here. We need to make sure we aren't leaving them empty-handed and stranded for the winter. It's going to start getting cold before long."

"I agree. I know they have horses and ducks...or at least they had one duck, but that won't get them far in the long run."

"Plus, I don't think they are going to be able to eat them if it came down to that. I know how attached you can get to your pets. We might be helping them by taking a few mouths to feed over the winter."

"It still doesn't feel right. They are just kids, and Harriette—"

"Harriette, what? Young man?" the woman said.

They both turned to find the trio looking at them.

"As touched as we are that you're worried about us, we are well prepared both with ammunition and seeds to keep ourselves and the animals fed over the winter," Harriette said. "You aren't going to talk us out of giving you the horses, nor are you going to talk us out of making sure you've got what you need to make it home."

"We just wouldn't feel right about taking them," Sarah said. "We didn't help the girls because we were looking to get anything out of it. Besides, you never know when you're going to need the spare horses."

"It's actually more helpful if you take two of them off our hands," Rose said. "We already ran the numbers, and we can make it through this with four horses, just not with six. You're actually saving them all if you take the two."

Sarah was blown away by their generosity. "I don't know what to say. It's definitely going to help us make it to Maine."

"You don't have to say anything," Harriette said. "Consider it a thank you for saving the girls and getting them back home safely."

Sarah smiled. "I wish it hadn't come to that, but you're more than welcome. I promise we'll take good care of them both."

"Do your parents have a barn or another building they can be housed in?" Rose asked.

"They sure do. They have a good-sized barn that would be perfect for them. Actually, we had a few when I was younger, but once they passed away from old age, we just thought it would be best if we didn't get new ones."

"As long as they help get you to your parents and they're going to be well taken care of, that's all that matters to us."

"They'll be in good hands at Harmony. My parents will probably be happy to have a few horses at the homestead," Sarah said. "I promise you have nothing to worry about when it comes to the horses."

"I have no doubt that you'll take good care of them. That's why none of us have any issue giving you the horses for your journey."

"Thank you so much. You have no idea what this means to us."

Before she knew what was happening, the girls were pulling her into a group hug. Sarah couldn't stop the tears from falling as she thought about how lucky they were. Now, they would be able to make it to her parents' place in half the time. With that knowledge dancing around in the back of her mind, Sarah was anxious to hit the road again.

"Now, dinner still has an hour before we can serve it, but I just put a pot of boiling water on the stove for a nice hot bath. Why don't you all go and get cleaned up and find a place to settle for the night. Then we can talk and get to know each other. I want to hear all about you girls and your adventures. For now, though, you can take these two to your mother's room for the night. I'll bring up some water for you shortly."

Sarah glanced at Adam as a blush jumped to her cheeks. She didn't want to argue with their host or seem ungrateful. Still, sleeping on the floor in the bedroom was better than the barn. If it came down to it, she was happy to crash on the carpet. As they headed into the beautifully built log cabin. The ranch-style home was open and inviting despite the chaos the world had collapsed into outside.

Walking through a large kitchen, the girls opened the

first door to the right, revealing a beautiful and large master bedroom and attached bath. Thankfully, there was also a small sofa in the corner that she was happy to take for the night. Looking around, her heart ached once again to be back with her own family. They would be leaving soon enough.

21

The next morning when she rose, she couldn't believe how well-rested she felt. Moving with the horses was going to change how they traveled. They couldn't travel at night any longer, which presented more dangers. Plus, horses were now of high value. If someone saw them, it was more likely they were going to be attacked for the animals. Once they reached her homestead, they could easily take care of the animals, but until then, they had to keep near fresh water.

Over the course of the night, they had used a map belonging to the girls' mother to locate a stream they'd be able to follow almost all the way to the small town just a few miles from the homestead. She was beyond anxious to get on the road and finally get to her parents. If they moved quickly and didn't stop for any reason beyond sleep and to give the horses a break, they could reach

Harmony Homestead in three days. Grabbing her bag from the bathroom, she glanced at herself in the mirror before heading out into the main part of the house where everyone had gathered.

She was finally going home. Smiling at the others, she took the coffee Harriette offered and listened as the others talked around her. It was nice to be a part of something larger, especially with everything so fractured in the world now. With every passing second she was awake, Sarah felt the road calling her more. Her parents weren't nearly as prepared with guns and youthful vigor. They needed her to get back to them. Fighting to keep her patience, Sarah tried to focus on what Harriette was telling Adam about the towns they'd be crossing through. The woman was a wealth of knowledge about the coast running to Canada.

"My late husband was a truck driver," she explained. "I traveled with him on and off."

"Are there any areas you think we should worry about in particular?" Sarah asked.

"Heading up north the way you're planning to go, I think the only place I would worry about is New York City. If it is at all possible, steer clear of the whole damn city."

"How much time do you think that will add since we're on horseback?"

"Honestly, I think it will take you about a day. Moving around an entire city like that is going to add some extra time, but at least you'd be alive to talk about it."

"How long would it take if we didn't go around?"

"You're looking at about twelve hours to go straight through, and that's on horseback. It will be too dangerous to take the horses, let alone yourselves," Harriette said. "People are going to be looking for an easier way to travel, and you'll be riding through one of the biggest cities on exactly what they're looking for."

"I agree with you about that," Adam said. "The people out there will do anything not to have to walk anywhere, and we've already run into some bad characters. Who knows what we'll find in New York."

Sarah knew they were both right, but the only thing she was thinking about was getting to the homestead and seeing if her parents were okay. The longer it took to reach her parents' home, the more concerned she grew about their well-being. There was no telling what they would run into along the way, and the fact that they were heading around one of the most dangerous cities in the world, was another thing she needed to worry about.

"Well, if that's the case, we need to head out as soon as possible. We're already running ahead of schedule, but I'd like to get there and check on my parents."

Sarah hadn't planned on cutting through New York City, but the idea had most certainly been dancing around in her mind. After all, she wanted to take the most direct route, but Harriette made sense. It was way too dangerous to go on horseback. On foot, they might be able to slip from building to building without being seen, but the horses made that impossible. The time they'd lose taking the long way was still worth taking the horses. They had cut their trip time in half despite detouring around New York City. The group quickly headed outside, where a gloom clouded the skies.

She didn't like the sight of the rainclouds but wouldn't postpone the journey because of them. Along with the trio of women, Adam and Sarah headed for the barn and started getting their horses ready. One thing after another was loaded onto the animals until Sarah was sure they had enough supplies to last them for a month on the road. When they led the two horses out of the barn, she felt her heart tugging at her once again. The three women had been so good to them. She hated leaving them there despite knowing how well they were prepared for the hard months ahead.

Turning to the others before climbing onto Ginger, Sarah wasn't surprised to find the two young girls ambush her into another embrace before she could get away. Despite how hard she fought them, the tears started falling again. After hugging Harriette and promising to check in on them after they got her parents settled in Maine, Adam and Sarah mounted up and slowly started to trot away from the farm. Sarah wiped the tears from her cheeks as Adam gave her a smile.

"Hey, is everything all right?" Adam asked.

"Yeah, I'm fine. I'm really worried about the girls and Harriette. I'd hate to see anything happen to any of them, but the girls are young, and even in this craziness, they have a lot of life to live still."

THE LAST HOMESTEAD

"Well, if it makes you feel any better, I promise we can come back and check on them once we get settled in at your parents'."

"Would you actually do that?"

"Do what?" Adam asked.

"Would you seriously ride back down through here with me just to check on these people?"

"Of course, Sarah. I'm actually having the time of my life right now. Between being with you and having this freedom—even with everything going on—feels better than I could have ever imagined."

"I didn't think about that part of it," Sarah said. "I know this isn't what you were originally expecting when you looked forward to being free."

"No, but I think this is better. No live television telling lies about me and no phones to keep everyone's attention from what's happening right in front of them. Plus, you've been a blast to hang out with and learn from."

Sarah smiled. "That's good. I'm really enjoying this time, too. I'm happy I'm finally going to get to the homestead. I look forward to seeing my parents."

"Well, for what it's worth, I look forward to seeing the homestead and meeting the people who raised you. I never thought this would be what my life would be, but I'm happy to see your parents' place."

"It's truly amazing. I think it's going to make you feel like you're right at home. I just hope we make it there with no other issues."

"We'll be all right. I trust your judgment."

They rode on in silence as the beautiful scenery unfolded around them. It was truly a fantastic morning for a ride. With the sun hidden behind the clouds, they weren't being burned in the sweltering rays like days before, nor were they chilled by the torrential downpour that had hit them on the second day of their journey. All Sarah could think about was getting home to her parents. She didn't want to think about how long it had been since they'd been without power. By her count, they were on day eight. The homestead was equipped with everything they needed to survive until power was restored to the world.

The ranch home had skylights throughout that made using lamps something they only did at night anyway. The large stores of propane, gasoline, and kerosene would already be filled thanks to her father's diligence, and the fuel would last a while given the now uselessness of the machinery they once powered. Wicks for her mother's antique lantern collection could quickly be made, and everything they grew was heirloom organics. What they didn't have, they could barter for and hopefully establish some reliable trading routes with the locals and villages.

She was excited to get home and get started, but the trepidation remained in her gut. They had been alone for eight days. Eight long days where anything could have happened. Her parents were old hippies—lovers and not fighters. If anything had happened to them because she'd taken too long to reach them, Sarah would never forgive herself. Gently putting pressure on Ginger's sides, she urged the horse to move faster. Sarah knew she wouldn't rest easy again until she was back at the family homestead.

22

Late that night, they reached the outskirts of New York City. She couldn't believe what a huge difference the horses made in the time they were making. Sarah didn't want to stop, not even to rest, but from where they were—ten miles from the city limits—she could hear gunshots ringing out. No matter what, they had to avoid the city and any chance of being found. They moved slower through the forest to cover their tracks. With the sun gone, they had no choice but to guide the horses with glow sticks on strings.

It was pure luck that she had them with her. Knowing they had to find shelter soon, Sarah continued to push her companion and the horses. The farther they could get into the forest, the better. Suddenly, there was a noise behind them, and Adam's horse spooked. The otherwise docile beast lurched forward with such sudden force that it knocked him off and galloped away before either of them could react. He hit the ground with a sickening thud.

Instantly, she was at his side, tying her horse to a tree before she helped him get to an upright position. He grabbed his left shoulder and gave a low hiss. Sarah could see that he was in a good bit of pain. As Adam cursed under his breath, she heard someone approaching in the distance and sprang to her feet, pulling out the gun she kept tucked in her belt. Whoever was coming didn't stop their approach as she cocked her gun and prepared to fire. Suddenly, George skidded to a stop, and she let out a breath of relief. He'd returned to his friend. Sarah tied off the second horse and went back to Adam, still sitting on the ground.

"Are you okay, Adam?"

"Yeah, but my shoulder hurts like a son of a bitch. I never imagined falling off a horse could feel like I got hit by a truck."

Sarah chuckled. "Yeah, well, you probably should have held on with your legs a little better."

"Maybe, but I don't think that would have stopped it from hurting like that."

"Let me take a look."

She quickly looked at Adam's shoulder and felt around the area. It didn't take long for her to realize why the man was in so much pain. Landing on his shoulder had caused it to dislocate from the socket. Sarah knew he wasn't going to like what needed to happen next. It had been a long time, but when she was a teenager, she dislocated her own, and the doctor needed to reset it. It wasn't a memory she was fond of.

"I hate to tell you this, but I'm pretty sure you dislocated it. I'm going to have to pop it back into place, or it's going to cause you a ton of issues."

Adam scoffed. "Great, sounds like it's going to hurt."

"Oh yeah, it's going to hurt like a mother trucker. At least it's not broken. That's something I don't think I could fix."

"Have you done this before?"

"Maybe once, but I promise I know what I'm doing. It's going to hurt like hell," Sarah said. "It could be worse."

"Fine, let's just get this over with."

"Just think about something else."

"What else am I going to think about?" Adam asked.

"Anything besides what I'm going to get ready to do. As long as it takes your mind off of it, it's going to work."

Adam sighed. "Her, at least the horse came back to us, right?"

"Yeah, lucky us," Sarah muttered.

As Adam started to chuckle, Sarah knew the moment had come. She had only ever popped someone's shoulder back into place once before, after her cousin had run his dirt bike into a tree. It had been sloppy back then, but she had learned from her mistakes. After that incident, she had taken several first aid courses and learned the proper way to set a dislocated shoulder. With one quick shove, she jolted it back into place, and Adam let out a colorful string of curse words. Sarah cringed, knowing it had to hurt worse than anything she'd ever felt before.

In the distance, she could hear the faint sounds of people approaching. She didn't know if they were looking for them or not, but they were close enough that Sarah could hear muffled voices. Despite the pain Adam was in, they had to keep moving deeper into the forest until they could find shelter. Then she would be able to do something about the pain. They had some medications in the bags, but she couldn't risk getting into them. Plus, if the people saw their glowsticks, they would give chase without question.

Snatching them off the sticks they were using as guides, she quickly buried them under some leaves and helped Adam to his feet. They couldn't ride in the dark without anything guiding their way. Sarah handed Adam the reins to his horse and motioned for him to be quiet as they moved forward. For at least half an hour, they moved without speaking, with only the clouded moon to guide them. She kept the sound of shots and the mayhem of the city to her right and the compass in her hand, using her lighter every now and then to ensure they were heading north.

Another half hour passed, and she saw what they were looking for, an abandoned hunting cabin in the middle of the forest. From the looks of it, it had been forgotten about long before the world went dark. The vines had worked their way up to the roof though it seemed to be free from holds if it started to rain. They quickly tied off the horses, and Adam took the lead as they stepped inside. It was dusty and dilapidated but would do for the night.

"Well, it doesn't look like much, but I think we can make do with this place for the night," Adam said. "What do you think?"

"Anything is better than trying to make our way through the mess out there right now," Sarah replied. "Are you hungry or anything? I can make us something."

"Right now, I can't think of much other than the pain. I don't even feel very hungry at the moment."

"I know. I just figured we could use something to eat. Here, take some aspirin. It should help with the pain, which I'm really sorry about."

"It's okay," Adam said. "I'm just really happy you knew how to do that and were able to get it back into place. I've heard horror stories about what happens when you don't."

"The sooner it gets put back in place, the better chance you have of healing. I just hate that it hurts you as much as it does."

"I'd rather deal with the pain than the alternative." Adam chuckled. "Besides, how'd you get so smart, anyway? You always seem to know what to do."

Sarah laughed. "You can thank my parents when we

THE LAST HOMESTEAD

get there. They taught me a whole bunch of things growing up."

"They were just looking out for you."

"I'm glad they did. They always told me a woman should be able to take care of herself no matter what situation arose. I'm not sure I believed them back then, but I'm glad they taught me the things they did."

"That makes two of us," Adam said. "I'm really looking forward to meeting them."

"It won't be too much longer now. I promise you're going to love the homestead."

"Oh, the more you tell me about it and them, the more excited I get."

As she went about setting up her bedroll for the night and getting out the horses' feed, Sarah thought about her parents. She never would have made it as far as she did if it hadn't been for them. They were everything to her. Once she was done getting herself ready for a few hours of sleep, Sarah grabbed the feed bags and headed back out to where the horses were tied. They had to find water first thing in the morning, but Adam needed rest. There was nothing else they could do so late at night.

By the time she finally managed to doze off, Adam was already snoring softly on the other side of the room. She was fascinated by him even after spending so much time together. Whenever she was with him, she felt herself at ease in a way she'd only ever felt back at Harmony Homestead. As the world started to fade around her, Sarah prayed her parents were safe and tucked in back at the farm. Without them in the world, she wouldn't know how to hold on.

Silently praying for her fears to dissipate, she listened to Adam's rhythmic breathing as she succumbed to her exhaustion.

23

It didn't matter how hard she tried to fall asleep or how exhausted she felt. Sarah was restless the entire night. After five hours of staring at the ceiling and listening to the thunder rolling outside, the sun finally started to peek over the mountains in the distance. At least Adam had gotten some sleep and would be rejuvenated for their ride that day. Sarah could manage without much sleep; she had been doing it for years. Listening to the leaves rustling outside, she tried one last time to doze off but couldn't get her mind to rest.

Instead, she sighed and sat up. There was something outside, a noise different than the normal rustling of horses and critters as they moved through the forest. Instantly, every one of her senses was on high alert. She listened quietly as she moved closer to the edge of the cabin. Her instincts had been spot on. With the new position, she could hear two people whispering right outside the cabin. She didn't know how many more there were, but she wasn't going to wait around to find out. Crawling over to where Adam was still snoring away, Sarah knew she had to be careful how she woke him.

If he freaked out, it might alert whoever was outside to their presence and awareness inside the cabin. They couldn't lose the horses. The packs on the animals had nearly everything they'd brought with them for the trip. Gently tapping on Adam's arm, she put her hand over his mouth as he jolted awake. In the pale rays of light that reached inside the cabin, his eyes flew open and darted to her. She motioned for him to be quiet and moved her hand as soon as he nodded in understanding. Adam kept low to the ground as she moved closer to whisper to him.

"There are people outside," Sarah said. "I don't know how many people there are, but I just heard two whispering to each other."

Adam reached for his gun, and she motioned for him to stop. If there was a chance that they could stop them without more violence, she had to try. For all she knew, they could be a couple of teenagers just trying to find their way in the new world. Luckily for her, he slowly took his hand off the gun and looked at her for direction.

"What are we going to do, then?"

"We have to get rid of the horse thieves without using our guns."

"Why would we want to do that?" Adam asked.

"Wouldn't it be easier to just dispatch them and get out of here?"

"Well, it's not just because of taking people's lives, but the fact that using the guns might spook the horses. Then, we'd be stuck trying to track them down. Gunfire could also attract other unwanted attention."

"Fair enough. You just tell me what we need to do, and I'll follow your direction."

"I'm going to try to do something. I need you to back me up. If you have to use the weapon, I will let you know."

"I thought you just said we weren't going to use them," Adam replied.

"I said we were going to *try* not to use them. There's still a big possibility they won't go quietly, and we're not going to let them get those horses under any circumstances. Just wait for me. I'll let you know what to do."

"Okay. I'm with you. How you want this to go, just let me know?"

Sarah poked her head over the edge of what was once a window but now only held rotting wood and broken glass. She could hear them over by the horses, but something stopped her from shooting. Despite her instinct telling her they were stealing the horses, she hesitated to fire at them or the animals unless it could be helped. As the sun moved a little higher in the sky, she saw who the horse thieves were for the first time and had to stifle a gasp. The two creatures couldn't have been older than ten.

There was a boy and a girl in tattered clothing with no shoes. They were whispering to each other as the boy tried to untie the knot she'd used on the horse's lead lines. Sarah had tied the knots intentionally, not wanting to make it easy on anyone who might want to take the valuable creatures. While her plan to stall them had worked, she was still shocked the culprits were so young. Adam gave her the same look of disbelief she knew was on her face. They still couldn't let them take the horses, no matter how small they were.

Creeping out first, Sarah pointed her gun at the distracted children but kept the safety on. As she slowly approached them, Adam moved away from her and through the trees to cut them off if they tried to run. Now that she was outside, Sarah could see the poor kids scarfing down everything they found in their packs as they worked on the knots. Had they not been starving, Sarah wasn't sure they'd have been distracted enough for her to approach without being heard. Her heart broke for the pair. Suddenly, a twig snapped under her foot, and they both jumped, spinning to face her as they did.

"I know you must be frightened," Sarah said. "There's no reason to be scared, so don't run away. Okay? I just want to talk to you for a minute."

They both looked scared to death, and Sarah couldn't imagine the fear running through their minds. She slowly lowered the gun just slightly, trying to gain their trust and also to let them know she meant them no harm. Both children moved closer to each other and watched her carefully as she tried to think of what to say. Her mind flashed back to when she was scared as a child, and she knew what she needed to do. Finding out who they were and what they were doing was the only way she knew to do it.

"What are your names?"

"My name is Jamie, and his name is Eric."

"Shut up, Jamie. We don't need to tell her anything. We don't know who she is, and she doesn't need to know anything about us."

"I don't want to hurt you. I just want to make sure you're both okay."

"I'm not afraid of you, lady," Eric said. "I know how to protect us, and I have a knife."

"There's nothing to be afraid of anyway," Sarah said. "I'm glad you have a way to protect yourself. I wouldn't want you to be out here all alone without a way to defend the two of you."

"You can't tell me anything that's going to make me trust you. We don't need your sympathy."

"Fine. You don't have to trust me. I just want you to know we're not a danger to you, and there's nothing to worry about. We are not going to hurt you," Sarah said.

"What do you mean *we*?" Eric growled. "Shit, Jamie, she's not alone."

Before she could stop either child from panicking, they both darted for the woods. Seconds later, she heard them scream, but before she could follow, Adam emerged with one child locked in each arm. They were struggling against him but weren't going to get free any time soon.

"What the heck are we going to do with them?" Adam asked.

"Well, we can't leave them here to fend for themselves. We've seen the sort of people who are out there. They have to come with us," Sarah said.

"I don't think either one wants that," Adam muttered.

Sarah sighed. She couldn't argue with him there. They were still trying to get free from him. If they were going to try to sneak away every second of the day, it was going to make the trip take three times as long. Sarah wasn't going to take them prisoner if they didn't want to be there.

"You're right. Let them go. They don't want to come with us to a place with unlimited food, safety, and the ocean just yards away; that's on them," Sarah said.

Adam shrugged and set both of them down. Instantly, Eric darted for the woods, but Jamie hesitated just long enough for her brother to pause and yell for her to hurry up. Her eyes met Sarah's.

"Are you some kind of creep?" Jamie asked.

Sarah shook her head. "Nope, we are going to my family home in Maine. They have a greenhouse, livestock, and a fishing boat. Have you ever had lobster?"

Now, both children were listening to her as she continued to tell them everything the homestead had to offer. By the time she was done, neither was in a hurry to leave anymore.

24

It didn't take long after feeding the children for Jamie to start opening up to them. Sarah watched in stunned amazement as the children ate their way through half of their supply. It was a heartbreaking story to hear. Jamie showed almost no emotions, though, as she shared how her mother had left them the week before the power outage. It was bad enough to think of a mother abandoning her children, but when Jamie mentioned they'd lived with her in an abandoned warehouse on the edge of the city, her heartbreak quickly turned to anger.

Whether or not the children knew it or not, from the way they spoke of their mother, Sarah knew the woman was frequently strung out on something. Now that the children were with them, she wasn't going to let anything bad happen to them ever again. Sarah wasn't sure what the future held, but the twins were now her responsibility and a burden she wouldn't take lightly. Still, she knew Adam had to be shocked by her decision to take the pair with them. As they loaded the horses back up, he pulled her aside.

"How do you want to do this? We are going to double our time if we try to walk all the way there again. Plus, we've only got two days of feed for the horses," Adam whispered.

"I know. We are going to double up on the horses. We'll try to give the animals a break as soon as we get on level ground, but until then, we need to get as far away from the city as possible. We've got to get to Harmony."

"Then I suggest we move out sooner rather than later. I don't like being stationary."

Sarah nodded in agreement and turned to the kids. They both looked excited and ready to get on the road, especially knowing they would be going on horseback. She had to admit the horses looked thrilled with the extra attention they were getting on top of everything else. She wasn't going to deny that simple pleasure to either the kids or the animals, given the state of the world. They could take a few extra minutes for some relaxation.

"How far do we have to go, anyway?" Eric asked.

"Well, if the two of you can stick it out for a little while, we'll be at the homestead by tomorrow night," Sarah said. "Do you think you can handle not stopping much?"

"I think so," Jaime said. "We're pretty tough."

Sarah smiled. "I bet the two of you are really tough."

"Are you guys married?" Eric asked.

"No. We're just good friends, and he's helping me get to my parents' house in Maine."

"How did you get to know each other?"

Adam laughed. "Well, Sarah worked as a security guard at a prison down in Florida."

"Wow, really?"

"Yep," Sarah said. "I worked there for several years and met Adam while I was there. We just hit it off pretty well, and we've been friends ever since."

"That's so cool," Eric said. "So, you're kind of like a cop?"

"I guess you could say that, in a way, I am just like a cop."

"What did you do before all of this, Adam?" Jaime asked.

The two were too young to understand when someone went to prison for something that they didn't do. As much as she believed in Adam's innocence, it wasn't the time to try to explain it to their newfound friends. She knew there was much they needed to learn, and Sarah had to find a way to change the subject.

"All you need to know is that he's a good friend of mine, and he won't hurt you," Sarah said. "Now, it's time for the two of you to hop up on the horses. We have a lot of ground to cover today, and we should probably get a head start on the day."

While she knew she couldn't keep his past a secret from anyone for long, she wasn't ready to explain everything at that moment. The conversation could wait until they got to the homestead. Then, she and Adam could tell everyone about his past and wrongful conviction all at once. Even with the added weight of Eric behind Adam and Jamie behind her, the horses seemed ready to hit the trail again. They lurched forward, and she was happy to have the sunlight to see her compass.

Moving north, they continued to make good time until she could hear the ocean and not the city any longer. She had slowly moved them closer to the water as they had moved away from the city. By the time they saw the water, she recognized the beach as one she'd traveled to frequently over the years with her family. Sarah's heart started to race. They were making fantastic time. If they pushed through the night, they could reach the homestead by daybreak. The sun was already started to move below the horizon as her horse stumbled forward onto the sand.

Sarah saw another lifeguard station ahead and thought fondly back to the first night they'd spent together. They had never done more than talk with each other, but the close bond she shared with Adam was there. Beyond the lifeguard's station was the pier another few hundred yards away. Even from where they were a quarter mile out, Sarah could see that the half-dozen storefronts had already been abandoned by their owners.

It broke her heart, but as the leader of the group, she was happy they would be able to pass beneath it without being noticed. As she looked on, Adam rode up next to her and smiled.

"Are you thinking about stopping there for the night?" Adam asked. "It looks like it has some good tactical advantages and cover from any passersby."

"Actually, I was thinking about riding through and making our way right by it. We're only a few hours away from the homestead, and I'd like to get us there."

"I know you would, and you will, but Eric is exhausted, and he's barely hanging in there as it is," Adam said. "Plus, the horses are already starting to stumble, too. We should stop for at least some rest."

Sarah knew he was right. As she looked at the children and then down at the horses, she quickly understood they all needed to rest for a few hours. None of them would make it if they didn't. Under normal circumstances and their original plan without the children, they would have made it with ease. The extra weight from the kids had exhausted the horses long before she had planned. Still, a little rest would be good for all of them.

"You're right," Sarah said. "I think we could all use some rest, and we can pick it up again when we're done."

"So, what's the plan then?"

"I think we should stop at the pier and give ourselves a breather."

"Will it be safe enough for us to stay for a little bit?"

"I don't know that anywhere is safe. With the way people have reacted to all of this, I'm not sure of anything. I just think it will be the best place to set up for the night."

"Well, your instincts haven't steered us wrong yet. I'm not going to question them now."

"It's as good as it's going to get until we make it to the homestead."

Sarah wasn't thrilled about stopping, but she knew Adam was right. She'd almost moved Jamie around to the front of the saddle a few times when she had started to doze. Hopefully, there were still rain barrels along the edge of the pier that the horses could use to get some fresh water. As they made their way closer to the pier, Sarah kept a watchful eye on their surroundings. She didn't see anyone right away, but that didn't mean they weren't hiding somewhere, waiting for the right opportunity to come along.

With three other people counting on her to keep them safe, Sarah was on high alert. She wasn't going to let them down; she wasn't going to let her parents down when they'd made it so far already. Moving at a slow trot, she stopped when they came to a shelter house twenty yards from the ramp that led to the pier. Slipping off her horse, she handed the reins to Adam and signaled for him to wait with the kids while she checked it out.

It didn't take long for her to visually confirm what she already knew. The pier and shops had been abandoned already. While they'd already been ransacked, at least the storm doors and windows would give them all a safe place to sleep for the night. Sarah smiled, knowing the following night they'd be safely back home.

25

She knew the others were exhausted by the pace she'd set for them the next day, but Sarah was determined to get to her parents. After another restless night of worrying about all of them, Sarah roused the others as soon as it was light enough to see out. They'd all gotten at least six hours of sleep which was more than enough. Now, with the homestead a mere two miles away, Sarah didn't want to stop. Their homestead was one of ten on the road leading to the small coastal community of McCafferty.

It wouldn't be long before others took up at the abandoned properties on both sides of her parents' places. They were the only locals still in the area. Everything else had been sold off to seasonal property owners, times shares, and rental companies. It came as no surprise to her that each plot of land they passed was as vacant as the previous. While a novice might consider expanding the homestead to a neighboring property, Sarah knew the ten acres her parents had would be more than sufficient for the number of people they had. Anything more and it would be too much for them to tend to and keep track of.

Her heart started to race when the homestead came into view. She wanted to gallop ahead and yell for her parents but knew if anything had happened and the land had been overtaken, she'd be giving the thieves a notice of their arrival. While the careless action might have been one, she'd consider when it was only her and Adam, with the children, she wouldn't dare. Instead, she brought her horse to a stop when the house came into sight and climbed down, again giving the reins to Adam. Sarah promised the trio she would be right back, but it wasn't enough for Adam.

"I don't like the idea of you going by yourself," Adam said. "We have no idea who is in there and whether or not your parents are okay."

"It will be fine," Sarah replied. "Besides, I need you to stay here and look after the kids in case something happens. I'm not going to risk them being thrown into the middle of anything."

"I get that, but I still would feel better if you had some backup."

"There's nothing to worry about."

"I don't know what's worse. The idea that you believe that or that you want me to."

Sarah sighed. "Look, I know you don't want me to go

in alone, but we don't have any other choice. I need to check out what's going on, but the kids need to know you have their back as well."

"I do, but from the looks of this place, it's entirely empty," Adam said. "It looks like it's been empty for a few days at the very least."

"I know, and that's why I'm worried. I thought they'd have this place up and running like there wasn't anything wrong, but it doesn't look that way. I'm just going to sneak around and see if I can see anything."

"Just promise me you'll be careful. We've already seen enough to know how bad something like this can be."

"I'll be careful. As worried as I am, I think everything will be all right. I just have to make sure before I subject the children to the unknown. You just take care of the kids, and I'll be right back."

"Watch yourself," Adam said. "I'll keep an eye on them, but I'll be looking out for you, too."

Sarah moved carefully and quietly while staying low to the ground and beneath the fence that ran along the road. It made her incredibly uneasy that her parents were nowhere to be seen. Even as she approached the front porch and looked inside, the house appeared empty. She cupped her hands over the window and gazed inside, but nothing looked out of place. There was a coffee cup sitting right next to her father's chair, where he always left it, and an open book by her mother's spot on the sofa. They had to be there. They had to be okay. Sarah needed them.

She could almost see them sitting there, talking about all the crazy things that had happened. Yet they weren't anywhere in sight. Her heart continued to race with each passing second as she moved around the deck to the side of the house. Still, there was no sign of her parents. They might not have been the youngest or the fittest, but they were smart and wouldn't hesitate to defend themselves if needed. She refused to believe something had happened to them, not after everything they'd done to reach the homestead.

The others had to be worried sick, but she had to find her parents first, no matter what state they were in. Around the back of the house, Sarah wiggled the door handles, but it was locked. She cursed under her breath. She looked around for the rock her parents had stashed the spare key under, but it was nowhere to be seen. Why would they move it unless they were worried about someone trying to get in that they didn't want? Panic gripped her as she fought to keep her head on a swivel.

Suddenly, she heard something behind her and spun around. "I thought I told you to wait with the kids," Sarah fumed. "What in the hell are you doing here?"

"Jamie got loose, and I couldn't hold her back. She was worried about you," Adam said. "Did you find anything?"

"I didn't really see anything, but I know my parents aren't here. I need to know what happened to them or where they could have gone."

"We will, Sarah. Whatever it takes, we'll find them. It's

been a really long trip, and the horses and kids are exhausted."

"I know. We need to take care of ourselves before we can figure out what happened to my parents."

"Exactly. I know you want to get this all figured out right now, but we are all really tired and hungry. The horses need to be fed, and so do we."

Sarah sighed. "Okay. Well, take the kids and horses down to the barn. I'll meet you down there as soon as I get everything situated, and we'll figure out what to do next."

"We're going to find them, Sarah. Nothing is lost. They just need to be found. There's any number of reasons they didn't stay here, and we're going to figure it out."

Sarah knew he was right. As much as her parents had tried to plan for everything, there were just some things that couldn't be planned ahead. She was thankful she had Adam by her side. Knowing her parents weren't there sent a shiver down her spine. Where could they have gone? Thinking about the kids, she started planning in her head how to take care of the group she now had.

"We'll find them, one way or another," Sarah said. "Thank you."

"No need to thank me. We're a team. Whatever we have to do, we'll do it together." Adam smiled.

Looking back through the window, she wondered if the best and only option was breaking through one of the glass panes on the door. She didn't want to do that.

Getting a replacement wasn't as easy as placing a call and waiting for a repairman anymore. Moving from one window to the next, she tried to find a way in without breaking anything but came up short. By the time she'd made a complete circle around the house and was standing in front of the back door again, Sarah was out of ideas.

She could hear the others laughing and carrying on in the barn behind her. Sarah was sure they were playing with the animals—a few goats and chickens, along with a handful of other barn animals. The horses would have good company when the trio finally made it back to the house. Fishing a pair of pliers out of her bag, she started working on the door. Ten minutes later, as she listened to them playing in the barn, she was still trying to break into her childhood home. When her hand slipped and her knuckles caught the jagged tool, Sarah cursed out loud.

"Now, how many times have I told you not to use language like that? See, Henry? This is what happens when you teach her such vulgar words at a young age," Connie said.

"Awe, hell, Connie, she takes after you with that mouth more than anything," Henry Fowler said.

Sarah gasped and spun around. Her parents stood a few feet away from her with two shotguns and a handful of slain rabbits between them. There were no words as joy overtook her, and she leaped from the porch and down the steps into her parents' waiting arms.

26

She never wanted to let her parents go again, as Sarah held them close. She couldn't believe her parents were home and safe. Of course, they were out hunting as if nothing had happened. In the minds of her elderly parents, having no power was no huge inconvenience. She was too happy about seeing them to be upset over their careless behavior. The only thing that mattered to her was that they were safe and sound. As she pulled away, she could see they were both crying as well.

Sarah couldn't imagine the fear her parents had gone through, wondering if their daughter would make it back home. Knowing they were both safe and well was all Sarah needed. There was time for a long, drawn-out welcome, and she could already see the children and Adam running in their direction to greet her parents. As they approached, Sarah turned her parents around to see the others. She could tell her mother was shocked to find two small children, covered in dirt and tattered clothing, along with the man still in his prison jumpsuit, jogging their way. Instantly, she grabbed Sarah's arm, but the younger woman quickly gave her a soothing smile.

That was all it took for Connie to calm down. Though she did lean closer and ask her daughter quietly who the people approaching them were. Before Sarah could answer her mother, her father gasped and muttered something about knowing the man and him being a danger. She didn't hesitate to lift a finger toward Adam, silently telling him to pause with the children for a moment. She had to let them know Adam wasn't a danger. Nor was he a threat to any of them there. It was quite the opposite, actually.

"Look, I know what the news reports said about him, but he was in my care at the prison for the entire time I was there," Sarah whispered.

"That doesn't mean you know the man," Henry said. "He was in prison for killing his girlfriend and unborn child, right?"

"Yes, but he was exonerated. Just before the power went out, I got an email from the prosecutor on his case. They had found all kinds of evidence that proved he couldn't have been the one who did it. I got it printed just before the storm took everything out."

"That's amazing timing," Henry replied. "Do you trust him?"

"I do, Dad. He's a good man who just deserves a chance at living a life that was taken from him."

"Well, if you trust him, then he's more than welcome to stay."

"I was wondering what would happen to the prison when all of this started," Connie said.

"We can talk about all of that later," Sarah said. "There's plenty to catch up on. Adam is going to be staying with us for now. I don't know what his plans are, and I don't think he does, either."

"Well, he can figure it out while he's here with us," Connie replied. "Where'd the children come from?"

"We ran into them on the way here. As far as I could tell, they were homeless, and it didn't seem as though their mother was worth much. They needed to come with us, and if I could help it, I wasn't going to leave them behind in that mess."

"I'm glad you didn't," Connie said. "Well, we have plenty of room at the homestead for them. They're welcome here."

Sarah was beyond enraged over the twin's life to that point, but she knew they had a good future ahead of them. Even with the world in complete turmoil. Waving for the others to come to meet her parents, they all met in the yard beneath the warm sun. When the introductions were done, her mother dove right into the role of caregiver and insisted on getting the kids clean. After promising them a trip to the ocean for an afternoon swim, they scurried away with Connie to find towels and food.

All the worries she'd had on the road faded away. There were still things that needed to be done, though, to make sure they continued to stay safe. She wasn't going to burden her mother or the children with any of that yet, but they were far from being prepared for the winter ahead. Granted, they would be able to save and use most of the crops they had grown, but they would need to find a way to get hay and feed for the winter.

"I know that look," Henry said. "What's on your mind, kiddo?"

"I was just thinking about everything we needed to do to get ready for the winter. We've got five more mouths to feed than we originally planned in case of an emergency."

"Five?" Henry asked.

"Yeah, three people and two horses," Sarah said.

Henry's eyebrows raised. Sarah could tell her father was both surprised and impressed by the revelation. Later on, she planned on telling him all about their interesting trip and the people they had met, but for the moment, she just wanted to make good use of what daylight they had left. Sarah jerked her head in the direction of the barn, and the trio started walking. She wanted Adam to know and be familiar with the property. It was his home now as well.

"Looks like the place is running like nothing happened," Adam said.

"Yeah," Sarah replied. "They've kept it running like clockwork, which is what I expected when we left Florida."

Henry chuckled. "We've been doing it for most of our lives, but it's going to be much easier to take care of now that you guys are here."

"What do you mean?" Adam asked.

"Well, now we have plenty of extra hands to help out around here."

"I'll be more than happy to put in my fair share of work. It will be nice to feel like I'm contributing to something, that's for sure."

"Now, there will be plenty of ways you can do that."

"Have you run into any real trouble since this started?" Sarah asked. "From what we've seen out there, the world is going to hell in a handbasket."

"We've had a couple of instances that caused us to have to protect ourselves, but it wasn't anything we couldn't handle. The world sure isn't what we thought it was."

"Did they try to take over the homestead or just try to steal from you?"

Henry sighed. "The first time anything happened, I think he was just stealing from the property. We offered him food and shelter, but he wanted more."

"So, what happened?" Sarah asked.

"We were talking and trying to reason with the man, but he charged at us. I fired a warning shot, but he kept coming. I had to shoot him to keep him from getting to us."

"I'm sorry that happened to you, sir," Adam said. "You said there was a second instance. What happened that time?"

"It wasn't as bad as the first, but it was a little more dangerous. There was a group of men starting to gather. I fired off a few pop shots to scare them off, and they went running. Other than that, there's been nothing else around here."

Sarah's gut churned. She was happy her father had been prepared for an attack but couldn't fathom how terrified the couple must have been to see men approaching. She was thrilled they were back there now and could help protect the homestead. Making their way into the barn, she took a deep breath and smiled. The smell of fresh hay and livestock always reminded her of home. The horses had been settled in a stall at the corner, the only free one they had at the moment.

Being back at the homestead felt like nothing Sarah ever could have imagined. It didn't stop the lingering worry she had for the friends she'd made along the way. Hopefully, Meredith was holding her own, and Alan had made it back to Becky and the kids. She wasn't as worried about Harriet and the girls. They were a tough lot. There would be time later for her to broach the subject of a trip south with the group later on. Before it was something she could consider, they had to make sure the homestead was secure and prepared for the winter ahead.

After they checked all of the fencing, they would be able to let the horses out in the small, two-acre pasture attached to the barn. It would work for now. With the livestock on the property constantly changing, she glanced into one stall after another to get a general head count of what her parents had on hand. Her father chuckled when he saw her doing this and shook his head. Sarah smiled back at him and rolled her eyes.

27

It was always a given that her parents would have chickens and turkeys. Since their roadside stand was open throughout Thanksgiving, people would vie and fight for reservations for the bird's years ahead of time. They would only raise a handful of them, feeding them with the same organic and homemade meals each night that the chickens got. Whatever their mother was cooking for dinner, the livestock was sure to get the leftovers.

Nothing on the farm went to waste. Everything from the produce that wasn't up to the standards of selling down to the manure that would fertilize the pastures to keep them green. Two deep wells on the property provided them with a constant influx of clean and potable water. Showering was going to be another matter. They had an outdoor shower to wash off sand and saltwater from the ocean, but it was little more than a hose attached to a showerhead. All of the plumbing would need to be rethought for the time being.

"You know, you haven't changed one bit since you were a little girl. You could just as easily ask me what livestock we've got, or do you doubt the old man's memory?" Henry asked.

"Dad," she groaned, "you are not that old, and your memory is sharper than mine."

"Man, you two remind me of my dad and me so much," Adam chimed in. "Why don't I break the stalemate. Sir, how many animals do you got here?"

Henry gave the man a wink. "Glad you asked, son. We've got two goats, two lambs, two kids—"

"Jesus, it's Noah's Ark," Sarah muttered.

"Two dozen laying hens, another dozen meat chickens, five turkeys, a cow and bull calf...and now two horses."

"And two kids," Adam added.

"Yeah, and those two now, not that we mind. Heaven knows we've got the room. They can take the bunkhouse room, and you two can take Sarah's—" Henry muttered.

"That won't be necessary, Pops," Sarah said. "Adam and I are just friends. We'll put him up in the guest room. Do you think anyone else will show up from the family?" Sarah asked.

"I don't think anyone else is coming," Henry said. "Both my brother and sister passed away years ago. "Their kids have all grown up and have families of their own. Places they call home. As much as I'd love to see them, I doubt they'd make their way here."

"That kind of brings up another dilemma, doesn't it?"

"What do you mean, son?"

"Well, if the time comes and there are more people who need help, we will be able to take on any more people?"

Henry sighed. "I think that's a conversation for another time. When we are all together, then we can talk about all those kinds of things."

Sarah chuckled. "My parents' marriage has been solid throughout the years because they always follow one golden rule."

"Yeah, and what rule is that?" Adam asked.

"They don't have any large conversations or make any decisions without doing it together."

"That's a great rule to follow. I don't think anything should be decided without first talking to the other person in a relationship."

"I'm glad you feel that way," Sarah said. "As long as we're here, none of us should make any rash decisions without first talking to the rest of the group."

Adam smiled. "I think I'm really going to like it here. After so many years of having all my decisions made for me, it will be nice to have some input on what happens now."

"You'll have your chances, Adam. I promise you, everything we do here will be something we decide as a team."

"Well, that's the tour," Henry said. "We should head back to the house. I think there are just a few things to show you on the way back."

As the trio headed back for the house, she pointed out different parts of the homestead to Adam. He was captivated by the greenhouse. Seconds before they reached the door, the kids burst out with towels in one hand and sprigs of soapwort in the others. They were quickly followed by Connie, who had a beach bag draped over her arm. She smiled when she saw the three adults approaching, but the kids reached them first.

"Will you guys come down to the beach with us?" Eric asked.

"Pretty please?" Jamie pleaded.

Sarah looked at Adam, unable to wipe the smile from her face.

"Awe, go on, you two," Harry said.

"Now you're not gonna get out of doing your mile today, either, mister," Connie said. "All three of you could use the walk. The planning and prepping can wait. We just got them back, Harry."

"Them?" Harry said. "I suppose I knew you'd make me a grandpa sooner or later. Reckon this gets us a jump start on the diapers and whatnot."

Sarah burst into laughter. "All right, we'll come down, too."

The kids gave a whoop of approval as they raced ahead of the adults across the sloping hill that led to the beachfront. It was a beautiful day for it, and Sarah knew the children would love life on the homestead. As they made their way over the top and looked out over the ocean and the beach below, Adam gave a low whistle.

"Tell me what you really think." Sarah chuckled.

"It's amazing. I don't think I've ever seen anything like it in my entire life. I can't imagine living in a place like this before all this started," Adam said. "Did you really grow up with this all around you?"

"I most certainly did, but don't let the allure of it all fool you. It's beautiful and heaven-like half of the year and like living in a hell the other half."

"I don't know if it could be that bad. Look at this place. No matter what time of year, I feel like it's an awesome place to be."

"Yeah, but in a couple of months, it's going to be freezing here. It's so cold at times that your breath will actually freeze in midair," Sarah said.

"Sounds like a sight to see, honestly. I'm all for new experiences, and I'm anxious to see how cold it really gets," Adam said.

"Well, just remember that it gets so cold that it could kill someone. It actually does almost once a year. This time of year, it's quite gorgeous, and the warmer air makes you feel like you would never want to leave. That cold winter air hits, and it's another story altogether."

"Oh, come on now," Connie said, appearing from out of nowhere. "It's not that bad around here. I think it's quite cozy."

Sarah chuckled. "You would be the one to disagree with me, Mom." Sarah chuckled.

"I think you just forgot how nice the winters can be here. The cold can get bitter, but the quiet nights are something to revel in."

"I might be with your mom on this one. Florida might have its perks, but I'm all about the calm and quiet."

As Sarah watched the three adults follow the children down to the beach, she couldn't help but worry all the same. She wanted to enjoy the moment of peace as much as they did, but she knew winter was going to be there in three months. Twelve weeks wasn't much time to be prepared. She hated the idea of postponing her trip back down the coast but didn't see how else they were going to manage it. Sarah started to do the math in her head. If she went alone, she could make it to Florida in seven days on horseback. It was still two weeks before she would be gone from the property.

Plus, she knew it was going to be a battle to get Adam to stay behind with the others and let her go by herself. Sarah could move faster, though, if she didn't have someone else to worry about, and she wanted Adam there to protect the rest of the group as well. As she started down the slope, Sarah wondered if it would be possible to get them completely winterized in ten short weeks. They would be able to do some of the work while she was gone, but she wouldn't leave without knowing the major tasks were already attended to for the pending cold.

Watching the children bound into the warm ocean, she smiled and let the worries slip away. Sarah knew how important the moment was not only for her parents but for the twins as well. She could already see that her mother was falling in love with the young children, and her father wasn't far behind. Hopefully, that bond would help carry them through the hardships Sarah knew were coming. Every day couldn't be spent at the beach. They had work to do.

28

After an exhausting but wonderful day, the twins were asleep before the sun went down that night. Sarah was leaning against the door frame of the bunkhouse bedroom that had three sets of bunk beds in it. It would be the twin's room for as long as they wanted it. Watching her mother tuck the blankets around them both, she couldn't help but feel her heart swell at the sight of the smile on Connie's face. She was truly a mother hen at heart. Sarah was positive she had made the right decision in bringing the twins with them. For the rest of their lives, the pair would have a family that absolutely adored them.

Tomorrow they would get a taste of true life on the farm. There was a lot of hard work to be done. She stepped aside as her mother entered the main living area and softly closed the bedroom door behind her. Connie was still smiling when she rolled her eyes at Sarah. It was a look of love. Sarah knew Connie adored the twins, and they adored her as well. Her mother linked her arm through Sarah's as they walked to the sliding glass doors off the kitchen that led to the patio.

Outside, Adam and her father were sitting on the back patio, looking out over the property. They each had a beer in their hand. Adam handed her a cold one. It came as no surprise to her that the bottle was still icy. The house was as old as the nation itself. Its deep cellar went back to its original builders, the purpose with the loss of electricity. Her mother had always kept a few bags of ice in the ancient icebox buried beneath the storage room. Now, Sarah was sure it was being used as a freezer and cooler. She plopped down next to Adam as her mother took a seat by Henry.

"What's on your mind, kiddo?" Henry asked.

"I was thinking it might be a good idea to take a full inventory of the supplies we have. That way, we can get a better idea of what we have before the winter months hit."

"I think that's a great idea, but it's something we should task the kids to do. There's going to be a lot of math involved with that, and it would be a good lesson for them."

Connie chuckled. "You're always trying to get out of doing math, Henry. I'll get started in the morning, and I'll go through all the dry goods we have."

"Not to be the one who brings up any of the awkward things during this time, but what have you been doing about going to the bathroom around here?" Adam asked. "I'm sure as nice as everything runs around here, the water isn't one of them."

Henry laughed. "It was one of the first things to go when the power shut down. No way for it to pump. We decided it would be best to dig a hole and put up a little outhouse down by the barn, but it won't last long."

"Well, if you'd like, I can build a bathhouse somewhere on the property," Adam said. "I build one quite a few years back, but I remember how to do it."

"Where'd you learn how to do that?" Sarah asked.

"My old man used to have a cabin off the grid. I spent a lot of time up there and built a bathhouse off the cabin."

"Well, I think that would work perfectly, considering the situation we're in now."

"I agree with my daughter," Henry said. "I think I know of the perfect spot for it, too."

"Great. Just let me know where you want it to go, and I can get started on it in the morning."

"We've still got a dollop of daylight left. Want to take a look now?" Henry asked.

Adam nodded as the pair rose. The mother and daughter watched them go. Sarah felt a little better, knowing they would start making progress in the morning. There were still a thousand more things for them to take care of, but at least she could check off one thing on the ever-growing list. She had no idea how they would do the harvest without the machinery. They would need to start on the orchard long before they normally would if the plan was going to be to harvest by hand. Thankfully, they had a few extra sets now.

"You know, your father and I have gotten spoiled with the furnace the last few winters. Don't get me wrong, we still use both of the wood stoves, but on those cold days, we have to kick it on," Connie said.

"Unfortunately, that's not going to be an option this winter, I don't think."

"So, you really think this is going to last for months?" Connie asked.

All Sarah could do was nod as the conversation fell silent. She didn't want to scare her mother, but she wouldn't lie to her, either. They all had to be prepared for what was to come. From what she had seen of the nation and what she had heard from others, they were going to be on their own for the next winter, at the very least. If power wasn't restored to the nation within a year, Sarah didn't know she would be shocked by that, either. Still, they had the twins to think about. Even if her mother could handle the reality of their situation, Sarah didn't want the twins to know about it just yet. It would take some time for them to adjust to life on the homestead. She wanted to take things one day at a time with them.

"I'd like to keep it from the twins, but I don't think we're going to have any help for a while," Sarah said. "If this is nationwide, we're going to be on our own for months, if not a few years."

"That doesn't surprise me much," Connie said. "The

government has never been very good at planning. Do you think we're safe here?"

"I don't know yet. There's still a lot that needs to be done to be sure we are safe for the winter, but I also need to scope out the area and go to town."

"What do you need from town?"

"Just to see what's left there and look for supplies," Sarah said. "I'll look for anything we could use and bring it back. I just want to make sure the kids are safe, as well as you and Dad."

"Well, what can we do to help make sure that happens?"

"Staying vigilant and watching everything we do will ensure our safety. We have to keep an eye on our surroundings at all times."

Connie smiled. "I'm really glad you came home, Sarah. I've missed you."

"I missed you guys, too. I'm just glad we made it and everyone is okay."

"I wasn't sure if you'd come. When I saw you with the others, I couldn't have been more proud of you."

"What do you mean?" Sarah asked.

"Well, you were able to find your way home, and along the way, you saved others. That's all I could ever hope from my daughter."

Sarah smiled. "I just did what I thought was right."

As the pair listened to nature around them, Sarah heard the sound of the men approaching the back patio again. Even as they entered, they were still engrossed in the conversation and what sounded like the blueprints for a really fantastic bathhouse. Sarah was happy the two were getting along, but new tensions would rise as they worked through everything as a team. Once again, her mind drifted to those they had left behind. With each passing hour, her promise to Meredith and the girls weighed heavily on her heart.

She had vowed to come back through and check on them. Meredith would surely need the help by the time she circled back. If nothing else, she could give the woman a way out of the prison and back to the homestead. The list of people who might need shelter continued to grow in her mind. She couldn't help but look out over the land as the sun faded beyond the trees behind them. There was room for another small house if they needed more room. Plus, a few neighboring properties had RVs they could use as second shelters. With the horses, they could get them there.

Sarah started making a mental checklist as her mother jogged to the grill and pulled off the boiling water she'd started for coffee. As soon as the smell wafted through the air, nostalgia struck Sarah. It was good to be home.

29

The next morning when she rose, Sarah felt like a completely new woman. She couldn't believe how amazing it felt to sleep in her old bed again. No matter what she did back at her apartment in Florida, nothing compared to your childhood home. She hadn't given much thought to what the small city she once called home looked like since the solar storm had changed everyone's lives. Sitting up in bed, Sarah stretched and looked out the window. It had to be at least nine in the morning.

She couldn't remember the last time she had slept so late without working the night shift. Instantly, she was on her feet and getting dressed. It was strange to think that she was now considered one of the lucky ones to have almost a complete wardrobe ready to go. How many people had been stranded at airports or on the road while traveling? It broke her heart to think of how many individuals were now struggling just to make it from one day to the next. As she headed out into the main part of the house and saw her mother plating breakfast, Sarah couldn't help but think of how domestic it all seemed.

The smell of bacon and the sound of it crackling over a grill could be heard through the open sliding glass doors. Somewhere outside, the twins were running wild and laughing with each other. She heard the sound of metal clanking against the hard soil and felt the subtle vibrations of the house. It sounded like her father and Adam were already starting construction on the new bathhouse. As she sat down at the island and smiled at her mother, Connie put a cup of coffee in front of her. It smelled like heaven.

"How'd you sleep, honey?" Connie asked.

"Well, I definitely slept a lot better than I have in a long time. I feel good about the day, and it was nice to sleep in a comfortable bed for once."

"That's good to hear. I'm glad you were able to get some rest. You looked exhausted yesterday."

"And now?"

"You look rested and happy."

"I am. This coffee is delicious, too," Sarah said. "How's everyone else doing this morning? How are the kids?"

"The kids are good. They've already fed the animals with me, and we walked the fence line to make sure there weren't any holes or breaks."

"What did they think about feeding the animals? I

remember how that used to be my favorite thing to do when I was a kid."

Connie smiled. "Oh, you loved feeding the animals. I think they enjoyed it. They really got a kick out of the chickens."

"What are they doing now?" Sarah asked.

"I'm pretty sure they're just waiting on breakfast, which should be done any time now. You look like you have something else on your mind, sweetheart. What are you thinking about?"

Sarah chuckled. "Is it always so obvious that I'm thinking about something?"

"I'm your mother, Sarah. I just know these things."

"Fine." She smiled. "I was thinking about doing a bit of a recon mission. I just want to get a look around and see how things are. If I can get a better idea of what's around us, then I will know how to protect us."

"Well, I think that's a great idea, especially since we have the kids here now. I don't want to see anything happen to them."

"I won't let that happen. I'm just worried about what Adam and Dad will say about me heading out on my own."

Her mother started to laugh and shook her head dismissively. Sarah knew Connie had more faith in her abilities than Adam or her father did. It wasn't their fault. They were simply protective over her by nature. Yet Connie understood just how skilled, silent, and crafty Sarah could be.

"Why don't you let me worry about them? But if you are going to go, I suggest you do so now before everyone comes inside for breakfast. It's going to be hot in a few hours. There's no reason for you to be out there in the heat," Connie said.

"I love you so much, Mom," Sarah said.

Connie grabbed a couple of slices of bread from the counter. "Go get yourself ready and make it quick. I'll fix you a breakfast sandwich for the road."

She was on her feet in an instant, racing around the counter to kiss her mom's cheek and give her a quick hug before rushing back to her room. She had unpacked everything from her bookbag the night before. Now, she only needed a few things in case of emergency. From her childhood closet, she grabbed the binoculars her parents had gotten her the Christmas before and the camouflage outfit she'd used for the last five years to go hunting with her father.

Sixty seconds after stuffing her gun in her belt and zipping her bag, she was jogging back to her mother in the kitchen. Connie handed her a sandwich wrapped in a paper towel before shooing her out the front door. There wasn't a minute to waste. Even as she slipped out the door, she heard the children and the men coming in through the creaking screen door in the back. Moving away from the house, she kept herself low and headed for the forest that separated their property from the next.

As Sarah slowly made her way through the woods, she started to think about the places she could go to check for supplies. She remembered the neighbors had a small RV. She wondered if they were still there or if they had taken off when all hell had broken loose around them. She couldn't blame anyone for trying to make it somewhere less open, but she would rather be able to see what was coming for her.

Memories she had made as a child came rushing back to her. Running through the woods with her friends, playing tag, and not a care in the world. Now, the world had changed, and she needed to constantly watch her back and look over her shoulder. Nothing had prepared her for the times they were in other than what her parents had taught her.

Finally, she made it to the neighboring driveway. Sarah stopped and looked around, but it didn't look like anyone had been there. The place looked entirely empty, but then again, so did her parents' house when they first arrived. She made her way from one side of the driveway to the other, but there were still no signs of movement.

Quietly making her way up the driveway, she reached the front door. The door was locked, but it didn't take much to pick up the lock and gained entry into the house. The first thing she did was to check the cabinets for anything that would be medically helpful. Painkillers and bandages were going to be needed, and she quickly found what she could.

Sarah had just started going through the medicine cabinet in the upstairs bathroom when she thought she heard a noise coming from downstairs. Instantly, her heart started to race. Trying to be as quiet as possible, she started to creep back down the stairs.

Moving down the steps, she tried to avoid the ones that had made noise on her trip up. Sarah pulled out the gun tucked into her pants and flipped off the safety. Despite still being able to hear them rummaging in the kitchen, whoever it was wasn't speaking. Suddenly, a loud noise emitted from one of the boards beneath her, and she cringed, pausing immediately. There was no way the intruders didn't know she was there now. The sound of quickly approaching feet made her jump the last few steps and spin around, ready to fire at whoever was charging her.

As quickly as she had the weapon pulled, she found herself holstering it again as the intruders attacked her. Sarah bent forward and picked up one of two obviously stray puppies as they wiggled at her feet. They were absolutely adorable, with scruffy and dirty brown fur from head to paw. With the RV she was looking for still parked in the driveway, Sarah considered the expedition incredibly successful. Checking the kitchen and the rest of the house one last time to make sure there was no puppy left behind, she tucked the pair into her bag and quickly headed back for the homestead.

The two would be a welcome addition, and she knew the twins would be in love with them as soon as they saw them. Hopefully, they would have more success than she had over the years at convincing Harry to let the puppies stay inside. Something told her the twins already had her father wrapped around their fingers. She smiled as the puppies wiggled in her book bag as she set out for Harmony Homestead with two more creatures to add to the arc.

30

Just as she had suspected, the instant the puppies were in the house, the twins were in love. There wasn't even a battle with Henry over them staying inside. He was like putty in the twin's hands. She had to back him up, though, when he insisted they take them to the well and wash them up before they came back in. Tasked with taking care of two living creatures, the twins quickly set about their work, plucking a few sprigs from the soapwort plant her mother kept on the patio in the process.

As an afterthought, Connie ran after them with two spools of twine to keep the puppies on a leash and to keep them from running away. With the men now fed and happy to go about their task outside, Sarah soon found herself alone once again. She wanted to take the opportunity and continue to scout the neighboring area. Many of the people in town were old family friends of theirs; Sarah had to know they were surviving without any problems. Grabbing her now-empty bag, she set what she had found at the neighbor's house on the counter for her mother and quietly slipped out the door once again.

This time her destination was in the opposite direction. She kept a steady jog as she made her way to the edges of town just a few miles down the road. Without knowing what to expect, she kept to the alleyways until she reached the main road. Moving along the brick wall of the locally owned pharmacy, Sarah peeked out at the courthouse and the rest of the village shops. The town appeared completely vacant, but she could hear people moving along the street. Until she knew if they were friendly or not, she wasn't going to risk exposing herself.

Sarah waited and watched for any signs of people on the street. Aside from the voices she heard, there was nothing to see. Suddenly, she saw a group emerge from around one of the buildings. Immediately after seeing the men come around from the side of the building, she noticed each one was carrying a gun. There were five men in total, and it didn't take long for her to figure out that she knew all five of them.

They were all councilmen of sorts. Running for public office. They all had that small-town look about them, and she knew they were all part of the good ol' boys club. Something that could be said about all countrymen raised in small towns. Since she knew who they were, Sarah thought about going and meeting them.

They would recognize her and might be willing to help in some way.

Before moving from the small safe area she was in, Sarah saw the old town drunk step out from the back of the group. She recognized the man. He was known for starting to drink early in the day and not stopping until he passed out in the street. He was mostly harmless, and she had some funny memories of the man. Sarah smiled to herself. If they weren't going to be willing to help, at least she could tell her family a funny story.

Suddenly, she noticed a rope around the drunk's neck and saw he was being led by a group of councilmen. He said something to the men, and one of them tugged on the rope, causing the drunk to fall. Another one of the men turned around, shooting the drunk in the leg. Sarah couldn't believe what she was watching. Instead of offering any help, the group of men all laughed, like he was some kind of court jester there to please the king. The sight sickened her.

Sarah was too baffled to process what she had just heard as she quickly moved back behind the brick wall. After what she had witnessed, she definitely did not want to expose herself to the group of men she had known her entire life. She started to creep back along the brick to the alley she had first emerged from. Sarah heard something behind her and instantly paused. Turning slowly, she found a woman standing at the back of the pharmacy where deliveries were normally made. Despite recognizing the familiar face, Sarah didn't move an inch. She had no idea anymore who was friendly and who was not.

The world had been completely flipped upside down. When Mary Carpenter ushered her over, looking around frantically to make sure the pair wasn't seen, Sarah was put at ease. She was obviously scared for her life, the same as Sarah suspected many of the villagers were with the mayor now apparently roaming the streets armed and dangerous. It was hard to believe that people she had once trusted with her life were now shooting innocent people. The man they had wounded was nothing the world would miss, but it still didn't justify what they were putting him through.

Torturing another human being, or any living creature for that matter, was simply not something she could condone. Even the animals they butchered back on the farm were done so in a humane manner. There was nothing humane about what the posse was doing. Sarah knew they were going to have to do something about it. As their footsteps and drunken laughter grew closer, Sarah had no choice but to take shelter with the woman now ushering her into the back of the pharmacy.

"Holy crap, Sarah," Mary said. "I can't believe you're actually here. It's been a long time."

"From the looks of it out there, I think I should have stayed away a little longer. What in the hell is going on here?" Sarah asked.

"It's been a shit show since the world went dark. The

mayor and his gang of douchebags have declared martial law."

"How can they get away with that?"

"What are we going to do to stop him? He's actually in control of everything here, and with the group he has with him, he has all the power. They've taken control of every part of our lives and run everything like some sort of game."

"Shit," Sarah muttered. "I don't have time to deal with this. I need to get out of here."

"Are you staying with your parents at the homestead?" Mary asked.

"Yeah. There's just a handful of us there, but there are a couple of children we're looking out for, too."

"Listen, I shouldn't be telling anyone this, but there has been some talk going around about them doing some kind of raids."

"What do you mean by that?"

"Well, since being shut off from the rest of the world, we've gone through a lot of our resources, and the mayor has talked about going out and finding more."

"Has there been any word as to where they will look?" Sarah asked.

"I'm assuming they will look at the nearby plots first before moving farther out to see what they can find. I'm only telling you so you can be prepared. Please, be careful."

"I will. Thank you for the information."

Sarah didn't want to believe what she was hearing.

There was no way the townsfolk would hurt her family. Even as she tried to dismiss the idea, Sarah remembered what she had seen moments before and knew it was a real possibility. The situation had been one that, admittedly, Sarah wasn't prepared for. She was now kicking herself for thinking the townspeople would work together in a time of hardship. Everything was different now. She couldn't leave, knowing danger was so close to them. What had once been a simple reconnaissance mission was now completely different.

They had to move quickly to get whatever they wanted from the local properties before the mayor, and his martial law posse moved in. On top of that, they would need to be prepared to defend themselves if the group tried to take the homestead. Sarah knew she could take the life of anyone who threatened her family, but how could she ask her parents to kill people they had known for over five decades? Thanking the woman one last time, Sarah poked her head out of the back door and listened for the men in the distance.

The coast appeared clear, and she didn't wanna waste any more time. Sarah darted back into the alley and raced away from the village at a sprint. The only goal she had now was to get back to her family and prepare them for what was going to happen. It wasn't going to be easy to convince her parents that the small town had fallen to the mayor, but they had to be made to understand. It wasn't just their own lives they were protecting now. They had the twins to think about as well.

31

Sarah didn't stop moving at a breakneck pace until the farm came into view. By then, she knew she hadn't been followed, but it didn't matter. She wasn't going to give her lungs a break until the family inside knew what was going on. Racing through the front door, she found her mother cleaning up from the morning meal, and instantly, Connie could tell something was wrong. When Sarah asked her to get the others and to tell the children to stay outside in the yard for a few minutes, Connie did what her daughter asked without hesitation.

It didn't take long for her to share everything she had witnessed with the others. With the plan already racing through her mind, Sarah didn't want to waste any time going over the details. They could take care of that later when they were out of daylight. Every minute now counted toward protecting the homestead and the people who lived there. She could see that her parents were completely shocked by the devastating news. While Adam didn't know the villagers like her parents had, she could see that he understood just what a baffling revelation the news was to them.

Sarah could sympathize with how they felt. It had been completely unnerving for her to witness it firsthand. Had she not, Sarah wasn't sure she would believe the men were capable of such terrible things. If what Mary had told her was true, they had a limited number of days before the gang moved out in their direction. They couldn't be wasting time reminiscing and questioning what was going to happen. Despite how anxious she was to get going, Sarah knew her parents needed a moment to deal with the shock.

"Are you sure the people you saw were the councilmen?" Henry asked. "It just doesn't make sense that they would do something like that. Hell, it doesn't make sense that the mayor declared martial law in the first place."

"I promise, Dad. It was those men, for sure. I wouldn't lie to you about what I saw there."

"Oh, I know. It just sounds like something out of a book."

"I know, but that's what the world has become out there. Evil is ruling things, and people like us are left defending themselves from it."

"So, what are we going to do now?" Adam asked.

"We need to start scouting the area. We don't have any time to lose."

"What is our first step, then?"

"You and Henry grab the horses and the cow," Sarah said. "Grab as much tack as you can find and meet me at the gate. I'll be there soon."

"What do you need me to do, dear?" Connie asked. "Whatever you need me to take care of, I'll make sure to follow your lead on this."

"Thanks, Mom, but for now, I think you should get the kids and keep them as close as possible."

"Should I keep working on things here, or should I take the children into the house and keep them there until you return?"

"Go ahead and keep working, but make sure you're keeping an eye out for anything out of the ordinary," Sarah said.

As an afterthought, Sarah realized they could no longer go around with just her gun out. Every single adult needed to be protected. If the children had been a little older, she would even ask that they be armed. As it was, she wanted an adult with a gun to stay with the children at all times. She wasn't going to risk their lives. Vigilance was going to be their best friend. Pulling her mother aside, she quickly whispered to the woman. She didn't care about the men hearing, but the noise outside had stopped, and Sarah suspected the twins were eavesdropping on the adults.

"Mom, I want you and the others to start carrying a gun with you at all times. Why don't you run to your room and get your shotgun and sling from the gun safe."

Connie pursed her lips. "Do you really think that's necessary? These people are our friends and neighbors. We've known them all for a long time."

"Mary Carpenter thought they were her friends, too, and now she is hiding and fearful for her life at the pharmacy. Do you want to be afraid, or do you want to be protected?" Sarah asked.

"Well, of course, I want to be protected. Don't tell me you want us to give the kids guns next?"

Sarah rolled her eyes. "Of course not, Mom, but you need to make sure they know there is danger out here right now. We are going to keep everyone safe, but we have to work together and watch each other's back to do that."

Connie said nothing in reply to her daughter, but Sarah could see her words had gotten through to the woman. She would be watchful of any strangers approaching the homestead, and for the time being, that was exactly what Sarah wanted. When they had more time, they could teach the kids to use bows and teach them to defend themselves, but for now, the adults having guns with them would have to do. When the group split up to take care of various tasks, Sarah felt the inklings of trepidation once again. They had to keep their property safe. Twenty minutes later, she was meeting Adam and her father with the horses and cow at the gate.

"So, what's the plan, honey?" Henry asked.

"We're going to raid the house for anything we can

use and load it all into the RV. You help me get it all to the RV, and I'll do the loading."

"What do you want us to do after that?" Adam asked.

"I need the two of you to find a way to get the horses hooked up to the RV. We're going to need them in order to haul the supplies back to the homestead."

"What about the cow?"

"Throw both of the saddlebags on the cow. We're going to use it for storage, too. Anything we find that will help get us by, we need to take with us."

"If we are using the cow for storage, what do we need the RV for?" Henry asked. "I doubt we're going to find that much to take in one home."

"Well, we don't know if anyone is going to come, and we might need to take on more if they do. I want to be ready if that does happen, and what better place for them to stay than an RV on the property."

"Once we get done at the house and bring everything back to the homestead, what are we going to do after that?" Adam asked.

"When we're done at the first one, then we'll move on to the next. We probably don't have a lot of time until they start trying to do the same thing we're doing. I'd like to beat them to the punch."

"Don't you think they'll figure out it was us eventually?"

"If they do, then we'll figure it out when the time comes," Sarah said. "Until then, we need to get as many supplies as we can."

The group set out onto the road, and a few minutes later, they were standing in front of the neighbor's small RV while the men worked on attaching the horses. Sarah took the cow and the saddle bags she carried to the front of the house and tied her off. The young calf played and grazed in the front yard while he waited for his mother. She set about getting the other supplies she had seen earlier in the day but left behind because of the puppies. Now, knowing the mayor was coming for the resources, she moved quickly throughout the house.

Along with several heavy blankets and cleaning out the kitchen, Sarah managed to get an abundance of extra medical supplies the owners kept on hand. Thankfully, there were no more live creatures that needed rescuing. She had to assume the mother was out wandering the woods somewhere. By the time she made it back outside, Sarah was impressed with the men's progress. Her father was already behind the wheel of the RV, and Adam was slowly leading the horses and the vehicle up the driveway to the road. After getting the cow loaded down, she followed after them.

Just a few hours after she had arrived back at the homestead, Sarah and the two men were setting out to find the next house and camper or RV they could take back to the homestead. She would be happy with one more, making a total of three dwellings for people to share if needed. As the night drew closer, her fear continued to grow that soon they would no longer be alone on the quiet road.

32

"Do you really think it will be enough? How many people are we expecting? We didn't find much ammo while we were out scavenging," Henry said.

"I don't know that we should be expecting anyone, but it's better to be prepared. As far as ammunition goes, I don't want us to have to kill anyone. I just want us to be able to defend ourselves and scare them away," Sarah said.

"Well, I don't know about your father, but I am happy to have you here helping out with all this. It's still hard to believe the mayor and the others could be behind something so ghastly as shooting an innocent man," Connie said.

Sarah shrugged but said nothing as she looked out over the main road. They had moved their now-nightly conversation to the front porch in an effort to continue to keep watch. The bathhouse was coming along well. Adam seemed optimistic that it would be done within a couple days. There was still a good bit of work to be done, but she was thankful they were making progress. Between the two trailers and the house, they could take on two more families of four if they needed to. Possibly even a couple extra stragglers if they were careful.

After going over the inventory list Connie and the twins had created, Sarah was pleasantly surprised that they would be well situated for the winter ahead. It would take them several weeks just to get enough dry firewood to last the winter if they wanted to outfit both RVs with a heat source as well, but between the four of them, they had all the necessary skills to do so. She knew that alone gave them an advantage over others now struggling with the new world.

"Do you think we need to have someone posted out and watching all night?" Connie asked. "What's to stop them from coming here when it's dark and trying to take what's ours?"

"I don't think that will be necessary. They never saw me when I went through there, and I don't think they'll do anything at night. They'll want to see what they're doing, and they won't be able to if it's dark."

"Still, I think if they want what we have, there won't be anything to stop them if someone's not keeping a lookout."

"Like I said, they never saw me. If they want to come here and look for what you have, they'll do it during the day. I'm sure they probably think it's just the two of you out here still."

"If we think they believe Connie and Henry are out here alone, shouldn't we try to keep up that appearance? Just in case they are watching over the properties around the area," Adam said.

"I think that's a good idea," Sarah said.

"How do we make sure they think it's just your mom and me here? Once they see everyone moving around, they'll know right away?"

"If they show up here, we'll have the two of them do the talking while we wait inside. I highly doubt they're keeping an eye out here. They've known you guys for years and probably aren't too worried about it."

"Well, at least we'll have the element of surprise on our side if they come," Adam said. "If they are just expecting your parents to be the only ones here."

"Yeah, but none of it is good right now."

"I wish it was different, Sarah, but we have to do what's best for everyone here. People are losing their minds out there. Even if we thought we knew them, we don't anymore."

She didn't love the idea of her parents being in the line of danger but knew it was the best way to prevent any bloodshed from happening. There was a good chance they would leave the homesteaders alone if the mayor thought they had nothing to offer. Still, Sarah had her doubts. They were well known throughout the area for their greenhouse and the orchard. Facilitating a trade route with the villagers would be the best bet, but she wasn't optimistic that the mayor would be willing to do so.

From what she had seen of the man, he was drunk on the power that martial law had given him. He wasn't the type of a man to be bargained with. They were going to be ready for him, no matter what the outcome of his arrival brought. It had been a long and physically exhausting day for all of them, and it came as no surprise when her parents stood and headed inside for bed. As tired as she was, Sarah couldn't pull herself off the porch. Her mother mentioning the men might come at night had triggered a protective instinct inside her.

While she hadn't planned on spending the night outside, her mind was quickly starting to change. If there was any chance that a night attack could come, she wanted to be ready for them. How a group of drunken men could still be awake at that late hour, Sarah had no idea. When she felt someone watching her, Sarah looked around and expected the worst but found Adam gazing at her with a smile on his lips. Instantly, she started to blush. They hadn't had much time alone since finding the twins. She didn't know what to say to him. So, much had changed since they had first met all those years ago.

"I don't know if you've noticed or not, but you're staring at me," Sarah said.

"Sorry, I don't mean to stare," Adam replied. "It's just that I can't get over how amazing you are."

Sarah laughed. "What do you mean?"

"I'm just saying. You really have your shit together when it comes to all of this. You're smart as hell and always know the right thing to do. I've never met a woman as smart as you are. Let alone how strong and resilient you are."

"You know, I might need to get you to put that into writing, just to remember you said it later on."

"Why do I need to remember that later?"

"I made a promise to Madison that I intend to keep. When I do what I promised her I would do, I'll need you to remember how smart you said I was."

"When do you plan on making good on that promise?"

As the question hung in the air, Sarah wasn't sure how to answer it. There was still a lot that needed to be done at the homestead before she could even think about going back. Still, a promise to her was worth its weight in gold. She had never broken a promise, and she wasn't going to start. No matter what happened at the end of helping her parents prepare, she had given her word to Meredith. Telling any of them was going to be hard enough, but putting a timeframe on it now was impossible.

"I haven't figured it all out yet, but when I do, I promise you will be the first to know," Sarah said.

Her friend fell silent next to her as they listened to the crickets in the forest. Sarah didn't know what to say to the man to comfort him. She wasn't going to go back on the promise she had made to Meredith. Still, convincing them that she was perfectly capable of going on her own wouldn't be easy. Sarah wanted to lay the foundation with Adam, knowing he trusted her and her instincts were a good start. It was getting late, and she could see the fatigue in his eyes.

"You need to go to bed. We have another long day ahead of us tomorrow," Sarah said.

"Oh yeah? And what about you? Are you going to sit out here, watching the road all night?" Adam asked.

Sarah grinned at him and shrugged. "I don't know. I'll probably come in a bit. I just want to stay out here a while longer and make sure it's all clear."

Adam chuckled as he rose, patting her shoulder as he walked by. "You really are something else, Sarah."

Her cheeks flushed once again as his hand moved away from her shoulder. Silence filled the air around her. Sarah prayed she was wrong about the villagers and her mother was right. The last thing she wanted was bloodshed when it wasn't needed. Despite the logic in her brain telling her there was nothing to worry about until the sun came up, Sarah still couldn't go inside as her eyes became heavy. As she dozed off in the chair, she thought about her parents and the people she loved inside the house. No one was going to hurt them on her watch.

33

Sarah woke the next morning, feeling like she had been hit by a truck. She stretched out and longed for the comfort of her bed, but the fresh layer of dew that covered her made her aware of the fact that she'd dozed off on the porch. The sun was barely starting to move over the horizon, and she was considering going to her room and crashing for a few more hours when she heard the front door open. Sarah sat up a little more, just in time to catch her father backing out of the door with two steaming cups of coffee in his hands.

He handed one to Sarah and took the seat across from her. Right away, she noticed he was doing what she'd asked and taking his gun with him everywhere. Setting down his coffee, Henry removed the shotgun from his shoulder and set it next to him in the chair. It was nice to see he was taking things seriously, even if he didn't want to believe his friends and local politicians could be capable of the horrors she had described. Hopefully, they would be able to come to some sort of terms with the mayor before there was any bloodshed.

Sarah knew that until that time came, she couldn't leave the homestead. It didn't stop the guilt from weighing heavily on her. Meredith had John working with her, but she didn't know how long they'd be able to hold the prison. If any of the good people there needed an escape, she was happy to help them find it. That couldn't be done from her parents' homestead in Maine. Turning her attention back to her father as she sipped the coffee, Sarah listened to the sounds of nature all around them. There was no denying that the homestead was a peaceful place unlike any other.

"So, honey, when do you plan on leaving again?" Henry asked.

"How is it that you and Mom both seem to have the ability to see right through me?"

"It's a parental magic power handed down once you have your first child."

"Well, I'm starting to believe that. You both always know what I'm thinking or that I'm about to do something. Sometimes you seem to know before I even know."

Henry chuckled. "There are no magic powers, Sarah. Your mom let it slip that you were planning to go back to help your boss. That woman never could keep a secret."

"Now, that makes more sense." Sarah laughed. "I don't know when I'm going to leave yet. There's still plenty to do here to get you guys ready for the winter first."

"I know I can't keep you from leaving, but I want to know you're going to be safe."

"I promise I will be careful when the time comes for me to leave. I know neither of you wants me to go, but I gave my word to Meredith, and I can't go back on it. No matter how shitty the world has become, our word is all we have. Probably more so now than ever before."

"Leave it to you to follow the lessons we taught you, even when we don't want you to." Henry smiled. "If you promised her you would be back, then you have no choice but to go back and help her."

"That's why I have to," Sarah said. "Still, there's plenty to do here that will keep me busy. I want to make sure you're well-prepared for the winter, especially since the twins are here now."

"They'll keep us busy, that's for sure."

Sarah fell silent. It felt good to be sitting there, drinking coffee with her father, as the world around them started to wake. She knew the children would still be asleep for several more hours, their little bodies slowly adjusting not only to having real nutrition for the first time but having a purpose in life. Suddenly, all of her senses started to tingle as she set down her cup and pulled out her gun. Her skilled eyes scanned the road in front of them. Off to the right, she saw a figure pop into the woods from where he had emerged on the road a few yards away from the edge of their property.

Instantly, she recognized him as a guy from town, but she didn't know the man on a first-name basis. She quickly whispered to her father to stay where he was as she raced off the porch and into the woods. She didn't want the man to see her coming. Minutes later, she could hear him tromping through the forest away from their homestead in the direction of town. She wasn't going to let him go, not given what she had heard the mayor say the day before. If he was working with them, she had to know.

Sarah circled around until she was in front of the man. Just a few minutes after she heard the guy in the forest, Sarah emerged onto the path in front of him with her gun drawn and pointed in his direction. Instantly, he froze, and the color drained from his face. He swallowed; his eyes darted past her. She knew he was thinking about running. To prove her point, she cocked the gun and leveled it at the man's chest. She wasn't going to let him go anywhere.

"Who in the hell are you, and what are you doing here?"

"I don't mean to intrude, but I'm from town. I'm just scouting ahead for the mayor. He asked me to look around to find out which houses are abandoned and which ones still have people staying in them."

"Well, we don't take too kindly to trespassers here," Sarah said. "Why don't you just tell me when they are coming?"

The man fell silent as Sarah kept the gun pointed at his chest. She didn't plan to kill the man unless he made a move of his own. Still, there were many questions she needed answers to, and she was willing to wait patiently for the answer to the most important one. If she knew when the men would be coming, they stood a better chance of stopping the mayor and the ones he brought with him.

"I want you to tell me when in the hell they will be here."

"They're on their way now. I don't know how long it will be," the man replied.

"You might not know how long it will take them, but I'm sure you have a good idea of how far behind you they are. So, tell me, where are they?" Sarah demanded.

"They're about two miles back. They're going house by house and scavenging for anything they can find."

"Good. See, that wasn't so hard, was it?"

"You have no idea what you're doing here."

"Maybe not, but I know when they're going to get here. Tell me, what are they going to do to you if you don't return and tell them what's ahead?"

The man scoffed. "Hell, they'll probably string me up and whip my ass."

"Maybe I should just let that happen. After all, you came onto our property."

Sarah heard her father approaching from the road and quickly holstered her weapon. If the man wanted to make a run for it, Sarah was confident she could stop him before it was too late. Her father looked from the man to her and back again. Sarah needed to get a plan in place with her father's help.

"So, what do you want to do with him?" Henry asked.

"We aren't killers, not like the others," Sarah muttered. "If we don't let him go back, they will know he's missing sooner or later."

"So, you want us to let him go? He'll just warn the others that we're here."

Sarah frowned, knowing her father was right. She didn't want to see any bloodshed, though, unless it was absolutely necessary. The best they could hope for was to strike some sort of deal with the mayor and his men. If it came down to it, Sarah would happily shoot every last one of them, but it wasn't her first choice for a diplomatic resolution.

"Go back and tell the mayor we're here and we are happy to talk with him. We aren't going to be bullied. I want to make that clear," Sarah told the man.

At first, he didn't seem to believe that they were letting him go. After a long pause, though, he darted off into the woods in the direction of town.

"Do you really think that was the best idea?" Henry asked.

Sarah shook her head. "Honestly, I have no idea. I want to believe there is a peaceful resolution, but I'm not counting on it."

34

Sarah knew they didn't have much time before the group arrived. Hopefully, they would be on foot though she knew having horses was common in the area. The mayor himself lived on a large estate on the outskirts of town, but as far as she knew, they didn't have any livestock. She couldn't imagine what his poor, docile wife was going through dealing with his power trip. Grabbing her father by the arm, Sarah quickly escorted him in the direction of the house.

The last thing she wanted was him out there while she was dealing with the mayor and the others. She wouldn't put his risk at life any more than she would the twins or her mother. Sarah questioned whether she should wake the others or not. She didn't want to scare them by the mayor's arrival, but she also didn't want them to be startled and come out in the middle of a tense negotiation, either. The decision wasn't hers alone to make. She needed to talk to her dad and see what he thought they should do as well.

The man had always offered her life-altering insight that sometimes Sarah was too bullheaded to see for herself. One thing she knew for certain was that they needed to get back to the house as quickly as possible. Any other conversations or decisions could wait until after that. Moments later, they emerged on the road in front of the homestead and quickly jogged back up the steps and into the open living room.

Her mother was now awake and smiled at the pair when they walked in. The smile quickly faded, though, when she saw her husband and daughter's expressions. Wiping her flower-covered hands on her apron, Connie quickly ushered the pair back outside onto the porch so as not to disturb the others.

"Tell me, what's going on," Connie said. "It has to be bad if the two of you both have the same look on your faces."

"We just caught a man coming onto the property. I stopped him and asked him what he was doing and who he was," Sarah said quickly.

"By stopping him, you mean you pointed a gun at him and made him give you answers?"

Sarah smiled. "You know I'm not going to let anything happen to anyone here as long as I'm around. So, yes, I threatened him, and he told me he worked for the mayor. Plus, he said he was scouting ahead to see what houses were empty."

"I take it they're going to be coming soon? The mayor and his men?"

"Yes. He told us they were a few miles behind him, so I don't think it will be too long before they get here."

"What are we going to do?" Connie asked.

"I need you to wake Adam. Have him help you with the twins and grab the guns to bring to me."

"What do I do with the children?"

"Well, it's basically morning time, and I'd rather they not be scared and worried about what's going on," Sarah said. "Go ahead and make them some breakfast, then take them down to the cellar. It will be safe down there."

"What are you going to do?"

"I'll figure out what to do. Just make sure the kids are safe and that Adam is awake. I'll fill him in on the rest when he gets here with the guns."

"All right, just be careful."

"I take it you've made your decision then?" Harry asked as Connie disappeared into Adam's room.

Sarah nodded. "I think the best course of action is going to be with a show of subtle force. I want you and Adam both on the porch with your guns, but I will be the one to talk to the mayor when he approaches. If anyone crosses off the road and onto that property line, I want both of you to shoot. I'm going to make that threat very clear to the men when they arrive, but I wouldn't be surprised if they questioned our resolve."

"Resolve? Hell, I'll shoot those sons of bitches for looking at me crooked if what you're saying is true and they shot an innocent man. Last I knew, being the town drunk wasn't supposed to be a death sentence."

"It's good to see we are on the same page," Sarah said. "I'm going to need you to keep that same mentality when the time comes. I don't know what we should expect, just that they're not the same people you used to know."

"No worries there. This is about protecting our own."

The conversation died down as Adam emerged from his room behind Connie, still rubbing the sleep from his eyes. As soon as he saw the worried expression on Sarah's and her father's faces, he was alert once again. It was a good thing, too; they were going to need all of the help they could get. It didn't take long for her to fill Adam in on what had happened. She was happy to see his expression instantly went to one of protective rage. She could sympathize with how he felt.

No one was going to take their home away from them. Time and time again on the road, they had witnessed people being less than human. That wasn't going to spill over into the life they had started to create at the homestead. She was ready to fight for their land against anyone who wanted to challenge them. Sarah watched as Connie ushered the sleepy children into the kitchen and listened for their footsteps heading into the basement. As her father emerged from his bedroom, she saw he was ready with two additional shotguns. He handed one over to Adam.

"Do you know how to use this thing, son?" Henry asked.

Adam chuckled. "It's been a pretty long time since I've been around anything like this, but I think I'll manage. My old man used to take me hunting all the time. It's been a while."

"Were you any good?"

"At hunting? Yeah, I did all right for the most part. I had a few deer heads hanging on my dad's wall."

"Really? You a trophy hunter, son?"

"No, sir. My pops was big on keeping the meat and using as much of the carcass as possible, but he said he was proud of me and paid a taxidermist for a couple of heads to be mounted."

"Good man. I was never one for trophies, but just remember, these are men with guns. They aren't going to run like a deer, but they might shoot back like a hunter."

"Just so you remember, we're just taking these guns as a precaution and for our safety. They're for protection. The plan is that we do this without having to kill anyone."

"I don't want to kill anyone," Adam said. "I will protect us from those men, whatever it takes."

"That's all we're going to do. Unless they choose violence. If they decide to go that route, I just need to know you're going to be able to do what will need to be done."

"Trust me. If they're coming for the property or anything on it, I'm going to put them down just as quick as they cross the property line."

"Good. Let's just hope it doesn't come to that, and we can resolve this peacefully."

As much as she wanted to hear stories about Adam's childhood, another noise piqued her interest outside. She raised her hand for the others to be silent as she listened. It was unmistakably at the sound of people approaching on the road and making no effort to be quiet about it. Drawing a ragged breath, she looked back at the others and gave them a nod of approval before setting out for the front patio. The men hadn't yet appeared in front of the homestead. She jerked her head, indicating Adam should stand on one end of the porch while her father took the other.

"You've got this, sweetheart," Henry whispered to her. "You could charm the skin off a rattlesnake if you wanted to. That fat tub of lard should be nothing."

She chuckled. "Thanks, Pops."

Sarah waited and watched the road for the group to emerge. As she did, she slowly started to take a step off the porch. Despite the churning in her gut as the first of the mayor's gang appeared, Sarah didn't let her unease show through. Her entire life had been one big test leading up to that moment. From working in the prison to taking martial arts, she was ready to defend her home and everything it stood for. As the mayor and his potbelly emerged, Sarah stepped onto the road with one hand resting on her gun and the other on her blade.

35

It came as no surprise when the large mayor meandered forward in front of the group of eight other men. Among them was the scout they had seen earlier in the day. She wasn't thrilled by how outnumbered they were but was confident her father and Adam were both better shots than the already tipsy posse of men. It was ridiculous to think of what their life had become. She felt like she was in an Old West film, waiting for a shootout with the bad guys. She couldn't take her eyes off the group. They were as untrustworthy as everyone else she had met.

Still, Sarah was curious to know if the mayor would admit what he had done or hide behind lies like a coward. Either way, she was ready to deal with him. The mayor's eyes moved slowly to the homestead and the men situated with weapons on the porch. She knew he was taking stock of what they had. It didn't matter. He wasn't gonna get his grubby, greasy, fat fingers on anything they owned unless he bartered for it. As much as she wanted to smack the smirk from the mayor's face, Sarah knew they had to play nice for as long as possible.

Reminding herself that her parents had a rapport with the man and his men, Sarah smiled and slipped her hand away from the weapon on her hip. If she could make the group feel less threatened, it would work in their favor. There were still things the homesteaders needed to make it through the winter, things that would be considerably easier to get through trade rather than trying to scavenge for them. Working as a team was the only way they would survive the disaster as a nation. Surely, the mayor had to see the good in forming alliances over killing in cold blood. In the new world, they had to work together if they were going to make it.

"How's everything going in the city, Mr. Smith?" Sarah asked.

"Oh please, Sarah, call me Douglas. Mr. Smith was my father's name. Overall, the city is doing fairly well. We're just pulling resources for the greater good."

"What are you trying to find?"

"Well, anything that will increase our chances of surviving," Douglas said. "Would you mind if we took an inventory of what you have on the homestead?"

Sarah didn't want them to know anything about what they had on the property, let alone a full inventory. She knew she needed to keep him interested in trading since it could be useful to both of the parties involved. As she looked at the man with a careful eye, she needed to know if they were just there to take what they wanted or if they were willing to work together.

"Listen, we're more than willing to work with you and trade goods and services, but you're not just going to come in here and take what you want."

"This is just how it works. The community comes together, and I provide what everyone needs."

"We have needs here, and we can take care of them on our own. I'm sure there are things we will need along the way, just like there will be things you will need. The best I can offer is to barter with you over the goods."

"If the community can just come together and pool our resources, it makes it easier to protect them from the outside world. I'm sure you've seen what's out there."

"I have seen what's out there, and we have no interest in being part of your plan. We're quite happy out here on our own," Sarah said.

She could see it wasn't the answer he had been looking for. There was an anger in his eyes that Sarah had seen before in some of the convicts. All of those men were still housed at the prison, convicted of terrible crimes. In that moment, there was no question about what she had witnessed back at the village. The mayor was a monster, barely veiled under the ruse of a kind-hearted politician. She didn't like the way the group was now staring around, nor did she like how the mayor was eyeing her family's homestead. Sarah was going to make sure he didn't get anything he didn't have coming to him.

"I know you have been away for a hot minute now, but I think your best bet let me talk to your old man. Why don't you go make us something nice and cool to drink?" he said.

Sarah glared at him. "I have a half dozen guns pointed at you and your men. I'm the one who speaks for my family. If you don't like that, I suggest you keep moving."

"You sure do have a smart mouth, now, don't you? Maybe it's time someone put you in your place, sweetheart," he said.

She didn't back down from the man, which was what Sarah presumed he had expected. Men like him didn't frighten her. Sarah had to deal with them every day back at the prison. They thought simply because they had the size, they were something to be afraid of. The reality was that Sarah could bring the man to his knees within seconds if she so desired. Taking a deep breath, she reminded herself that they were trying to make progress without violence.

"Listen, as I said, we're willing to barter for anything you need. Just tell me what you're looking for, and I'm sure we can come to some kind of terms."

"I'm not looking to trade, honey. I want to know what in the hell you have in there so that we can work together for the better good."

"I'm not letting you take an inventory, but if we have what you need, we can work it out," Sarah said. "So, here's what is going to happen. You're going to offer us a trade, or you can keep it moving along. We have things to do."

"Or we can just come in there and take a look around. I'm sure you won't mind once you remember how things work around here."

"Well, you can try to make a move on my family or this property, but if you were to do that, then you would be the first one we take out."

Douglas sighed. "I don't think you understand what you're doing, Sarah. I have men who would take them down before anything else could happen."

"I understand you have men who will do anything you tell them to do. Hell, they'll probably be willing to die for you if you said the word," Sarah seethed. "But I guarantee you that you're not willing to put your own ass on the line in this situation."

She watched as Douglas's jaw clenched, and he looked around. It was easy to see she had upset him, but he had no choice but to listen to every word she said. She could tell that he was thinking about the possible outcomes, and when he spat at his feet, she could see he felt defeated. Even if it was just temporary, it was still a win.

"Fine, I'll send someone over to barter with you people."

As the group of men brushed past her to raid the houses and farms farther down the road, Sarah let out the breath she had been holding. She couldn't believe the confrontation was over. She didn't need the feeling in her gut to tell her it wouldn't end so smoothly the next time. They hadn't heard the last of the mayor. At some point or another, he was going to make a play for the farm, and she knew it. Just like they had been that morning, they would be ready for him and his men.

The way he had looked her up and down stayed with her as she slowly retreated onto the property. Sarah wasn't going to turn her back on the men, not even with Adam and her father pointing guns in their direction. They needed to be prepared for whatever came next. She could guess the mayor wasn't going to be happy when he saw the other homes had already been raided as well. Their entire morning had been a waste of time. Sarah wished she could see the look on the mayor's face when he went to the next few properties and found them void of anything he needed.

They had gone as far as cleaning out the liquor cabinets. The alcohol could be used to soothe their nerves but also for cooking, preserving, and medical use in the future. When the men disappeared down the neighboring driveway, Sarah finally turned back to the others and jogged up the porch steps. Her father and Adam quickly put her at the top.

36

As the days turned to weeks without any confrontation from the villagers or their beer-bellied leader, Sarah started to feel like everything was getting into a normal swing. It had been four weeks since they had reached the homestead, but so much had changed. The bathhouse had been finished within days and now was a favorite spot for not only Sarah but her mother as well. The men had gone above and beyond in creating it. From the skylight to the steam room, it rivaled some she had only seen in gyms. It was amazing what they could do without electric or power tools.

The twins had found a happy rhythm and routine with Connie, who adored working with them every day. Between her father teaching them the ways of the homestead, Adam teaching them how to take care of themselves, and Connie teaching them everything a school might, they were destined to be incredibly well-rounded children. Sarah knew their lives would have been incredibly different had they never crossed paths. Despite how well everything was going, she still had the nagging feeling in her gut that they needed to head south to check on the others.

They hadn't heard anything from the villagers beyond the few who came to the homestead to trade with her parents. The mayor hadn't again set foot on the land, nor had any of his men. From the gossip that traveled to the homestead with the tradesmen, Sarah knew the mayor was still enraged over what he saw as direct disrespect. She loathed the man with every ounce of her body. Given the opportunity, she would have enjoyed exacting some martial law on him herself. The nights were starting to get chilly as the adults gathered on the porch after the twins had gone to sleep.

They had done just about everything possible to be prepared for the harsh coming months. While the weeks had been busy and full of progress, the only thing that remained out of stalemate was her relationship with Adam. They had flirted and even gone as far as professing their feelings, but they still had almost no time together alone. There was an understanding between the two, an unspoken bond neither was in a rush to define. After all, they had all the time in the world.

Her heart raced as she looked out over the land. With all of the adults there, there was no reason for her to procrastinate telling them what she was planning any longer. She couldn't believe how nervous it made her. She was a grown woman with nothing tying her down, so to speak. Yet the obligation she felt to check on Meredith and the girls was deeply rooted inside her. Sarah had to leave, and everyone she loved deserved to know it was coming. Taking a deep breath, Sarah smiled at her mother before starting the conversation.

"I need you guys to know I'll be leaving in a couple of days to head back south," Sarah said. "Everything here is all set for you and the incoming winter months, and I made a promise to check back with Meredith as soon as I could."

"We knew it was coming but didn't realize it would be so quickly," Adam said. "How long do you think you'll be gone."

"Honestly, I don't really have any plans on how long I will be gone. I wish I could tell you for sure. I'd say it shouldn't be more than a few weeks."

"Well, do you think it's possible for us to talk you out of it?" Henry asked. "I hate to see you go. You've seen what's out there for yourself."

Sarah chuckled. "No, not even a little bit of a chance. I have to go back to check on Meredith. I can't break the promise I made to her."

"Yeah, I know. I was only hoping there was a chance, but I completely understand the need to make good on your word. Plus, it's nice to have the extra set of hands around here. It makes things a lot easier."

"Well, if it makes you feel any better, Adam is going to

be right here the whole time to make sure everything is taken care of. He'll be able to keep an eye out and help with anything you might need."

"Why don't the two of you leave her alone?" Connie chuckled. "She's made up her mind, and she knows what she's doing."

"I just wish my daughter would take someone with her. It's not safe out there."

Sarah didn't want to have the familiar argument again with her father. It was always the same thing, only the circumstances changed. He hadn't wanted her to leave when she first went to Florida, either. It had been her mother's insistence that had kept him home and forced him not to follow her and check in when she left. Now, Sarah knew she needed a little of her mother's magic to help get her on the road. It wasn't something that she could stop. Sarah had to make sure the others were okay.

"Honey, just leave her be," Connie said. "She'll be just fine out there by herself. We've taught her everything she needs to survive, and she's tough like you, Henry."

"Thanks, Mom."

"You're welcome, dear. Just promise us that you'll be safe and come back to us in one piece."

"I promise I'll take care of myself. Besides, I've learned everything from you."

Adam chuckled. "You should really have a ton of faith in your daughter. She made it just fine getting up here, and I know she can do it again."

"That's right. She got all the way here from Florida

and brought three wonderful things home with her. She'd going to be fine, dear," Connie said. "Now, leave the girl alone so she can take care of the promise she made."

"Fine, but I don't have to like it," Henry said. "I'd feel a lot better if there was someone going with her."

"I know you don't like it, Dad, but it's only going to be for a few weeks, and then I'll be home."

"Okay, but watch your ass out there. These people are ruthless and don't care how many people stand in your way."

"I'll be careful, Dad. You showed me what I would need to do to get by when this day came. Now, I'll use everything I know. Just make sure you're all keeping an eye out for our old friend, the mayor."

Adam smiled. "I planned on it." Adam smiled.

"Good, because I still don't trust him not to come to try something, and since I won't be here to protect you—"

"But I will be here, Sarah," Adam said. "I'll keep a lookout for Mayor Smith and his goons. They won't get onto the property without a fight; even if he does, I'll put him down. Your family will be safe."

Sarah was certain the closer it got to winter, the better the chance was that the mayor would show back up. He likely wasn't prepared for the cold months ahead. His people, though, were terrified into submission and would be asking about how he planned to get them through until the spring came. A desperate man was a dangerous one. The faster she could get out of there and get back home again, the better. It wasn't that she didn't trust Adam and her parents to keep things safe. She would simply feel better if she was there to keep an extra watchful eye over things.

* * *

Two days later, as Sarah tightened the girth on the horse before climbing on, she heard the children running out to tell her goodbye before she saw them. Connie yelled after them not to run around the horse, but her scolding did little to stop them. Sarah was delighted they had all found their rhythm. She was going to miss each and every one of them while she was on the road. Despite knowing what she was doing, Henry went around and double-checked all of her gear before he finally circled back to the horse's head and gave his nod of approval. Sarah wasn't going to say anything to him about it.

She knew her father was just worried about her. After giving her parents, the twins, and Adam an embrace and farewell, Sarah climbed into the saddle and set off down the road. She couldn't resist looking back one last time as the farm disappeared out of view to wave at the children still waiting at the end of the driveway. Sarah's heart already ached to be back with them, but she knew she had a job to do. Pulling her father's compass out of her pocket, she headed south one last time.

37

Sarah made it to the girls' homestead in record time. Just as she had suspected, a solo rider was far easier to maneuver around the country than a group or even riding with a partner. It didn't take longer than two days for her to get to the girls and Harriet. As soon as her horse saw the familiar landscape, she felt him getting excited beneath her. Every step became a prance as he fought against the bridle. She could understand how he felt. For almost two weeks, she'd had the same anxiety about getting back to her own home.

A part of her had hoped the horse would consider Maine his home now, but she couldn't blame him for being excited. The property looked a little different, though, as she approached. Right away, she saw they had fashioned a bathroom outdoors along with a kitchen. Sarah wanted to make sure she didn't scare anyone as she approached and carefully brought her horse to a walk. She understood how much he wanted to get back to his home and his old friends, but there was no guarantee the girls were still there.

For all she knew, they had been overrun by people leaving the city and were now on the run. It didn't take long for her to realize that was not the case unless they had left behind all of their animals as well. Several horses trotted to the gate to greet their old friend as she dismounted. Seconds later, a large dark dog started to bark at her, and a man emerged on the front porch. Instantly, her hand was on her holstered gun. Suddenly, Harriette's familiar face emerged behind the man, and she quickly scolded him to drop the shotgun he was pointing at Sarah. Harriette yelled back into the house for the girls before racing in Sarah's direction.

As she watched Harriette moving in her direction, she noticed the girls coming up behind her. Bella and Rose looked exactly the same as the day she had left them. Sarah was glad to see Harriette and the girls were good and well. She looked past the girls. She quickly grabbed a glimpse of a woman she didn't know, stepping out of the front door and onto the porch.

"Oh, my God, Sarah," Harriette said. "I can't believe you're actually here. We've been wondering if you'd stop back by at any time. Heck, just the other day, we were talking about it."

"Did you make it to your parents' home?" Rose asked.

"I did, and everything is set up for the winter. Just making a trip back because of a promise I made."

"That's good to hear."

"How are you?" Bella asked. "Tell us everything you know about being out there and how your trip was."

"I'm doing good, and the trip was good, too. There's plenty of time to tell you all about that," Sarah said.

"We want you to meet our parents."

Grabbing her arms from both sides, the girls directed her to the porch, where a man now stood next to the woman she had seen standing on the porch. Sarah was happy to see the girls happy and excited, and she followed them onto the porch. After a few introductions and handshakes, a question popped into her mind that couldn't be controlled.

"I didn't know you were married. The way the girls explained it was that you were a single mother, and you had a boyfriend."

Marsha laughed. "Well, when we left on the cruise, Josh and I weren't even engaged when we left, but we decided to tie the knot while on the ship."

"Congratulations," Sarah said. "How were you able to do that with everything being the way they are now?"

"Oh, we did it on the ship. Got married and all the paperwork right before the world went to hell."

"Girls, why don't you take the horse down to the barn and get him fed," Harriette said. "I'll go in and grab the scotch."

After much insistence from the woman, Sarah took a

seat on the front porch along with the girl's mother and their new stepfather. She couldn't believe how much had changed in the short time they had been separated. Still, Sarah couldn't think of a better outcome for the two young women. It was obvious they were thriving and happy on the homestead. The couple seemed happy and pleasant enough, but Sarah still felt awkward trying to get to know someone, given their current situation. The circumstance was a tense one, though they always were for someone like her who had social anxiety.

"You know, my girls talk about you all the time. They talk about you like you're a hero," Marsha said.

"I'm not a hero. Just a woman who likes to make sure others are safe."

"That's a hero in my eyes," Josh said. "Besides, even if that weren't the truth, you saved those girls, and we can't thank you enough."

"He's right. I can't thank you enough for what you did for my daughters."

"You're welcome. They're good girls," Sarah said. "How did you guys make it back here?"

Marsha laughed. "Let me tell you, it was one hell of a trip."

"That's putting it mildly," Josh said.

"Well, we were kayaking off the coast of Mexico when the lights went out. We had to go through a lot to even make it back across the border."

Sarah smiled. "I figured they would have all the

borders closed when the power went out and the world went to shit. How were you able to get back?"

"We've only been back for about a week. We got stuck with all the legal aspects since there wasn't a real way to make sure our documents were valid."

Josh chuckled. "We went through a bunch of crap to even get a place to stay while we were there."

"If it weren't for the friends Josh has in the Mexican government, we probably would still be stuck in Mexico, waiting to get across."

As Sarah listened to Josh tell her about his humanitarian work not only with the Mexican government but also with the Cuban government, she felt her mind starting to drift away. It wasn't that his story wasn't interesting; it simply didn't matter anymore. There was only one thing she wanted to know about: the state of the world outside of the small corner she had seen. She listened politely for a few more minutes before finally getting the opportunity to interject and ask the question that had been nagging on her mind.

"So, you have seen a lot more of the country than we have. How are things looking?" Sarah asked.

She didn't need her gut instinct to tell her what the look the two exchanged meant. It wasn't good. Still, she wanted to know what was going on. No, she *had* to know what was happening. As nice as it sounded to live in the dark, it wasn't a path for her. Especially since she was not returning right home but instead heading farther south.

If she could spread any news or developments with others, Sarah felt obligated to do so.

"Honestly? It's not great news. It's not even good news. Actually, there simply is no news. Everywhere is dark. A few places have power back, but it's all solar and was incredibly well protected. We are talking like... fifteen locations generating a small amount of solar power," Josh said.

"Well," Sarah muttered, "I guess something is better than nothing, right? And fifteen isn't bad in the grand scheme of things. Are they all localized? Like we had a base set up somewhere?"

They both looked at her with matching expressions of confusion, but it was Marsha who spoke.

"Oh, I think you're a little confused. Fifteen places... on the planet. We've heard Switzerland has the most, but it's such a small scale that it won't power even a city of fifty people. The US was working on two solar projects and the rest...well, I don't know where they are."

Sarah swallowed. "Holy shit. We are going to be in the dark for years, aren't we?"

"Who knows, but I do know this winter, we are going to see a side of humanity we've never seen before. You guys should be prepared for that. When we were getting back into the country from Mexico...it was terrible," Marsha whispered.

Sarah's gaze darted to Josh. He shook his head and took his wife's hand.

"There were men and women on the border...just

shooting at anything, anyone that tried to cross. We saw them execute men, women, and children. It was awful," Josh whispered.

Sarah swallowed, her stomach churning as the words hung heavy in the air. Maybe her father had been right. Maybe Sarah should have taken someone with her to travel down the coast. The world was changing.

38

She wanted to stay and spend more time with the girls and their family, but the road and the safety of her own home called to her. Heading south to Meredith was her last stop. By the next morning, Sarah was ready to head out with her horse already loaded down for the long journey ahead of them. After hugging the girls and their housekeeper goodbye, they set off onto the road. She had no intention of sticking to the beach, given their trip up the coast. Keeping to the roads but avoiding the main cities was her plan.

For four days, they traveled as much as possible. Sarah pushed herself and her horse from the time the sun came up until it went back down again, but by the fourth afternoon, mere hours before the sun started to set, she saw the prison coming into view ahead of her. Her mount must have felt her tensions from the trip ease as they approached. Moving to the front gate, she saw the guard in the tower and waved. She wasn't sure who it was, but they waved back before signaling to someone near her old block.

Almost immediately, she noticed something was off as she looked around the yard. There was no way Meredith would let it become as trashed as it now looked unless they were desperately short on staff and inmates. Despite the churning in her stomach, she continued to smile as a man jogged in the direction of the gate. He gave her a friendly wave. While he was wearing a guard's uniform, Sarah instantly recognized the man as one of the inmates. George felt Sarah's tension and took several steps away from the gate as the man opened it.

"What can we do for you?" the inmate asked.

"Tell me where Meredith is?"

"Oh, she's inside working on a project. As you can see, the outside of this place has been pretty much left alone, and that's because we have so much to do in the building."

"I thought she had planned to work the garden and the inner parts as a whole," Sarah said.

He smiled. "Well, that was the idea until a few weeks ago. Had a few things go wrong and we've kind of been stuck working on…other things." He smiled.

Sarah could tell the man was lying to her. Though he was well versed in his deceptive tactics, she knew Meredith would never let the garden go to waste, and her friend wouldn't ever allow the mess that now surrounded her. While there was no way to be certain of what had happened, her only concern was where Meredith was now.

"I'd like to talk to her myself," Sarah said. "You know, just to make sure everything is all right. I promised her I would check in on her and make sure she was doing okay."

"She's doing just fine, actually. Yeah, she has everyone working hard and taking care of things."

"Well, she can take a break and talk. Will you have her come out, please?"

"As I said before, she's pretty tied up at the moment. You're more than welcome to come on in and see how she's doing."

"No, just have her come out to see me. I'll wait."

"I'm sorry, ma'am. That's just not possible." He grinned. "Safety concerns and all that."

"She'll let this one pass. Now, I'll wait right outside the gates for Meredith. Have her come out to meet me."

The man snickered. "Fine, suit yourself."

His eyes darted to her right as he opened the gate wider. George was starting to prance beneath her as she quickly looked around to see what the man was looking at. Suddenly, five men emerged from the forest, positioned roughly fifty feet apart. It didn't matter what direction they bolted; the inmates would have time to get to her. She wasn't going down without a fight. Giving George his head, she squeezed her mount's sides and let him bolt in what his survival instincts told him was the best direction.

As he lunged to the right and galloped along the fence, she quickly pulled out her gun. Shots rang out through the night as Sarah cursed and returned fire. Of course, the inmates were armed. She hated herself for leaving Meredith behind, but it was obvious the prison had fallen. Sarah didn't just recognize the inmates in the forest; she knew they were all dangerous men who were supposed to still be behind bars.

Suddenly, a searing pain coursed through her right side just below her ribs. She screamed out and grabbed her side, tugging on George's reins to guide him into the cover of the forest. Her palm was hot and sticky as soon as she pulled it away from her side. Sarah had been shot. There was no way she could risk stopping and letting the men catch up to her, but she could feel the blood dripping down through her fingers and onto her leg.

They'd only been in the forest for a few minutes when George stumbled over a tree limb he hadn't seen and nearly went down. Sarah cringed in pain and brought him to a stop before carefully climbing down. She wasn't going to risk his life by letting him stumble through the dark forest. She knew the area well enough to know they were heading south, and at that moment, that was all she cared about.

"It's okay, George," Sarah whispered. "Well, I guess it's kind of not all right. I guess we're in some deep shit now."

As she led George through the woods, she couldn't help but wonder what had gone wrong. Had everyone else at the prison left Meredith by herself or had the inmates simply overpowered the remaining guards and taken over? Sarah planned on figuring it out, but first, she needed to get herself to safety.

Thoughts continued to rush through her head, and the blinding pain was making it harder to walk. She didn't know how far she was going to be able to make it, but she continued to push forward. Within a few minutes, Sarah began to feel lightheaded and sick. The world started to spin around her, but still, she kept herself and George moving. She wanted to put as much distance between herself and the prison as she could. Suddenly, she remembered a place they could go that wasn't too far away. As long as it was still standing.

"George, there's a place just a few miles away. It's an old campground that used to be an amazing place to go," Sarah whispered.

It had been a while since she had gone in that direction, but it was the only place she could think of that might be safe for the both of them. The pain was still taking its toll on her, and she knew they needed to keep moving. While it felt silly, talking to George was helping her to stay awake.

"We can make it there if we keep moving. We're just going to have to keep it slow and quiet." Sarah chuckled. "Thanks to you, George, we're going to get away from here and figure out what the hell is going on."

Sarah knew it was a ridiculous thing to be talking to the animal, but it brought her some comfort as they walked through the treacherous forest. Thus far, she hadn't heard anyone following them, but she'd gotten a good head start by having a horse. If their inmate files were any indication of what the men would do to a woman, she wouldn't feel safe until there was a wall and locked door between them and her.

Plus, there wasn't a chance in hell that she was going to leave George outside wherever they stayed. After all, there was no one around to tell her the horse couldn't come into whatever abandoned house she found. Her stomach rolled as the stench of blood stung her nostrils. Not knowing how bad the wound was, she couldn't tell if every step she took had a purpose or not. From the way it felt, she could have been bleeding out and never known. Why had the prison fallen? Had someone betrayed Meredith, or did they simply overthrow her and the other guards somehow?

Sarah had to get down to Alan and find out what had happened. He was only twenty miles away from the prison, making it an easy trek if she were able to bandage herself up. Every step brought her more pain and closer to the edge of collapsing until she was leaning against George for support. Just when she was sure she could go no farther, the abandoned cabins of the campgrounds came into view. They were small and primitive, but they would do for the night. Praying for a little more strength to get them through the doors, Sarah started to climb the cabin's three steps.

39

Sarah cursed as she shrugged off her bag and tied George to one of the bunk bed posts. There wasn't much room, but they would be safe for a little while until she planned her next step. Every time she moved, pain shot through her side as she pulled up her shirt and inspected the wound. Thankfully, the shot had been a through and through. Another inch over, and it would have hit her internal organs. If that had been the case, George would be on his own and never make it back to either of his homes. Sarah wasn't going to let that happen.

Fumbling through her bag, she found the liquid stitch she'd packed for George and quickly squirted it over both sides of the wound. It really needed stitches, but she didn't have the time, skills, or tools. She'd be lucky if it didn't get infected or she didn't bleed out. Pressing down on the wound to help the stitch hold, she quickly

THE LAST HOMESTEAD

wrapped a bandage around her waist to keep the gauze in place. Finally, she sat back against the wall and drew a ragged breath. She was exhausted and covered in blood.

Given the wildlife that lived near them, she didn't want to stay in the blood-soaked clothing for long, but she couldn't bring herself to move from the chair. All she wanted to do was go to sleep for a little while. Her body needed time to heal; it needed rest. Every voice in her head pleaded with her to stay awake, but she had never felt sleep pulling her with such ferocity before. It had to be the blood loss. Slowly the world started to fade around her until she heard George nickering across the room. Sarah groaned but rose slowly and moved to the bed beneath where he was tied.

"Well, George, I think I really messed up this time. I just don't know how much longer I can hold on. I'm so tired. Maybe I'm not going to make it," Sarah muttered.

While her brain was still trying to process the situation and work through her feelings, her eyes became heavy. She tried to force herself to stay awake, but sleep called to her like a wild animal in the night. There seemed to be no way to fight it off. Suddenly, she felt George nudge her, and then he nickered. Sarah knew she wasn't alone and that George would have her back. She chuckled lightly at the thought of George fighting for her survival.

"I'm sorry, buddy. I'm just so tired right now…

Sarah was slowly starting to lose consciousness. She continued to fight the feeling of exhaustion, but it didn't seem to be of any use. It was only a matter of time before she passed out, and there wasn't anything she could do to stop it. Her mind rushed through some memories and random thoughts as she fought off sleep. When George nudged her again, she jolted and looked into the eyes of the horse which had carried her such great distance.

"Thanks, George," Sarah muttered. "Listen, I know you're trying to take care of me right now, but if I wake up and you've eaten my arm or something, I don't think we can be friends anymore."

Sarah chuckled lightly. While horses were more known for eating hay and other things, it was even lesser known that if they got hungry enough that they would eat meat as well. The thought was almost comical to her now. For a few seconds longer, she fought off the darkness. Within a minute of laughing, Sarah could no longer stay awake and gave in to the sleep that awaited her.

Sarah rose hours later, feeling like death had tugged her close to the edge. Had it not been for the incredible animal nudging her incessantly, she might not have come back around at all. Her body felt like it was on fire as beads of sweat rolled down her forehead. It was chilly outside, even in Florida. As soon as she was back in the world of the living, Sarah could hear something outside the cabin. It had to be why the horse had tried so hard to wake her. With danger approaching and no way to flee, the horse's instinct was to seek help.

Despite knowing they had to get out of there, Sarah struggled to move. She grabbed her side and hissed when she pulled away her hand. The bandage was holding, but it still felt like she was being shot over and over again. Something was definitely wrong with the wound, but there wasn't time to think about it. The only thing Sarah needed to focus on was getting her and George as far away from the approaching people as possible. Stifling a groan of pain, she pulled herself to her feet and grabbed George's reins.

It took every ounce of willpower to get her bag off the ground and looped over the horn of George's saddle. While she knew it was a terrible idea and could fall off at any point in the forest, Sarah's options were limited. She couldn't even think about getting it onto her shoulders. Trying to walk was challenging enough. She didn't know how she was going to get them both out of there without being noticed by whoever was now stalking them at the edge of the campgrounds.

Sarah quietly and quickly loosened the reins that held George in place for the hours she was asleep. Moving herself and her trusty steed through the cabin, they made their way to the door leading them out. The entire process took less than a minute, but the searing pain and the unknown now lurking outside made it feel much longer. She could still hear the movement and light voices around her, closer than they had been moments earlier.

Suddenly, she felt the gravel beneath her feet. They were right where they needed to be, and Sarah felt a rush of relief. Nothing had been certain when they had rushed from the prison, but she knew they were moments from freedom once the rocks moved under her. The path was theirs for the taking, but they had to be careful.

George was leading, aside from a few readjustments along the way. Her head was still fuzzy, and the pain was beginning to get to her, but she knew the only way they would survive was to keep moving. Trying to stay as silent as possible, Sarah kept the pair pushing forward down the path. Though her heart was racing, she understood she could keep them both safe from the dangers around them if they just stayed on the path.

Though they hadn't stopped moving, the voices and sounds of the people searching behind them continued to grow louder with every passing moment. Sarah knew they needed to push forward. Any stop would only allow the followers more time to close in on them. She was still fighting through the pain and trying to keep her head from spinning, but they weren't going to stop.

They had to move faster. She couldn't let them be caught by whoever was following them. As close as they still were to the prison, Sarah was certain it wasn't friendlies just looking for a place to stay. Sarah had spent enough time around inmates to know when they saw a pretty woman—or any woman for that matter—they could and would do dangerous things. Sarah wouldn't ever paint the entire inmate population in that same color, but the ones they'd deliberately left locked away were being kept there for a reason.

The men running the prison were not friendlies. The wound draining her life was proof enough of that. The footsteps and muffled voices were slowly starting to grow closer to them, but she wasn't going to let them take her down. Pulling George to a stop, she knew what needed to be done. If they were going to get out of there alive, they needed to go at George's best pace. That meant she needed to get into the saddle so he could carry them both to safety.

It pained her to reach for the horn, and despite trying to keep her weight off the wounded side, Sarah still gasped in pain when any weight at all was put on it. Even after she let go of the horn, the renewed sharp pain in her side stayed on. Sarah was struggling to catch her breath as she gripped her side. Even though it was dark all around her, she could still feel the world spinning. Sarah stumbled, still keeping hold of George's reins as she collapsed onto the hard gravel. There was nothing she could do; she was slipping into unconsciousness. No one would be saved because of her.

40

Sarah woke hours later groggy and aching but not nearly as bad as it had been before. Right away, she was aware of the fact that she no longer had a fever. Her heart started to race instantly, though, when she heard the muffled voices of people around her. One side of her body still felt warm, but one was fine. Opening her eyes, she had to blink against the harsh light of a campfire. At least it explained why she felt like she was on fire over half her body. She tried to move but could barely sit up without the world starting to spin around her.

The whispering stopped, and she saw a figure approaching from the other side of the fire. She tried to get away, but it was no use. She was still too weak. All around her, the camp had fallen silent. She didn't like that she was now the center of attention. That could only mean one thing with a gang of roving, lonely, dangerous male inmates. She had to find George and get away.

"Hey now, take it easy, Sarah. You're with a friend," the figure said.

Her eyes slowly started to focus and adjust to the light. When the familiar face came into view, Sarah sobbed with joy. It was no monster coming to violate her. Without giving her wound any consideration, she lunged forward and wrapped her arms around her friend.

"Oh, honey. It's okay now. You're with friends. Whatever happened to you out there, it's not going to be able to get you in here."

"I'm just happy it's you, Becky," Sarah said. "How did we even get—"

The realization struck her that they were still in danger. Whoever had been searching for her had to know where they were. Two women and a horse would be a perfect target for some of the evil people of the world. Sarah knew she had to protect her friend from whatever had been hunting her down.

"We need to run, Becky. There are people looking for me, and I don't want them to get to you."

"It's okay, Sarah. We're hidden away here, and there are miles between us and the jail. They won't be able to get to you here. I promise."

Sarah sighed with relief. Although she was still worried about their safety, she knew Becky wouldn't lie to her just to make her feel comfortable. The pain was still there but nowhere near as bad as it had been when she had lost consciousness. Whatever happened at the prison was still at the forefront of her mind. She suddenly realized that while Becky was there by her side, she hadn't heard or seen Alan.

"What about Alan and the kids?" Sarah asked. "Is everyone all right?"

"They're all here and safe. We've been thinking about you, and we're happy to see you're alive. We didn't know if you made it to your parents' homestead."

"I made it and got them prepared for the winter, but I made a promise to check in with Meredith, but when I got there, the inmates were in control. I need to find out where she—"

"She's here, too," Becky said. "Meredith is here with us."

Sarah was too blown away to speak as the tears started to roll down her cheeks. From the other side of the fire, Meredith appeared along with Alan and all three kids. She couldn't believe what she was seeing. Meredith was at her side in an instant, carefully wrapping her arms around her friend from the prison as she softly cried. Even in the dim light, Sarah could see the bruises on Meredith's cheeks. She felt a surge of rage coursing through her despite the persistent pain in her side.

"What the hell happened to you?" Sarah asked.

Meredith glanced back at the children and shook her head. "We can talk about that later. What matters is that you are safe with us. You're alone. Did something happen to Adam?"

"No, he's at the homestead with my parents. I came back down to check on you."

"So, that's where the wound came from. I was wondering if that was the case. I'm happy that's all that happened."

"When did they overthrow it?" Sarah asked.

Again, Meredith glanced back at the children. Sarah could see she didn't want to talk about the events at the prison. She mentally kicked herself for asking about it again. There was so much more she needed to know. To start with, it was still too dark for her to recognize any of her surroundings. If she was going to get them all back to the homestead, Sarah had to get her bearings. She tried to sit up again and did so with a little more success the second time around despite Becky and Meredith both telling her to lay back down.

It didn't matter how far they were from the prison; she wouldn't feel safe until they were in Maine. There were questions she needed answered. Thankfully, she could hear George softly nickering a few feet from where she was lying near the fire. At least she knew he had made it out of there with them as well. Sarah could never forgive herself if the beast somehow had gotten left behind.

"How did you all end up together?" Sarah asked.

"Well, some of it started about a week ago," Alan said. "It's kind of all a mess at this point."

"What do you mean?"

"A group of thugs came rolling through our area

roughly a week ago. It didn't take long for them to overrun the whole place. We made a run for it, and I thought the prison would be a safe place. After all, Meredith had a good plan for running it."

"I'm sorry you lost everything," Sarah said. "How'd you meet up with Meredith?"

"People have lost more, that's for sure. Just as we got a little closer to the prison, Meredith caught us and told us what had happened. We've been moving ever since."

"I'm really glad you all found each other. It's not easy being alone out here."

"That's for sure," Alan said.

"We don't have any idea where we are going to go. Everything has been taken over by thugs or groups of people who want nothing more than to treat people like garbage," Becky said. "We just know we have to stick together now."

"We've got each other," Alan said. "That's the important thing. Like she said, we have no idea where we're going to go, but you're welcome to join us in our search."

"Well, one thing I know for sure is that I'm glad we're all together. I wasn't sure if I'd ever see any of you again."

"We're all here now. We'll find a place that is safe."

"There's no need to go searching for anything. I know of the perfect place, and that's where we're going to go together," Sarah said. "The homestead has plenty of room for you all."

The group was blown away by her revelation, but she'd planned on them joining her from the first moment they'd moved RVs. Somewhere in her heart, Sarah had known they would all come back to the homestead with her. She only regretted not asking them to join her sooner or at least not forcing the issue. From the wounded look in her former boss's eyes, Sarah didn't know what she had been through before escaping the prison and finding the others. An hour later, as Becky and Alan tucked the kids in around the campfire for a few hours of sleep, Meredith moved to where Sarah was sitting just out of earshot from them.

"Hey, how are you feeling?" Meredith asked.

"Better with a registered nurse keeping watch on me," Sarah replied. "What about you?"

She sighed. "Still recovering mentally, but I'm physically okay."

"I'm so sorry for whatever happened to you, Meredith. I should have stayed longer. This is all my fault."

"Don't blame yourself, honey. There is nothing you could have done. If it hadn't been for John, things would have been worse, but he got me out before they did more than get in a few sucker punches."

Sarah gasped. "John made it out with you?"

Meredith cringed and shook her head. "A few of the other guards were still there, being held by the inmates. He stayed behind to get them."

"We have to go back," she whispered. "We have to help—"

"Sarah, we can't. It's overrun. There are more than just the prisoners there now. Others have joined up.

They've taken control of the forest ten miles around the prison, and they're moving into the cities. John is the only one who can stop them. He's on the inside, and the leader's second in command. Winter is setting in, right? Your family…"

"They need me," Sarah said with resounding confidence.

41

Becky refused to let the group move out while Sarah was still healing. By the next afternoon, Sarah was becoming agitated with their lack of movement. Despite their location twenty miles north of the prison, she didn't feel safe given what they now knew about the complex. It would have to be a problem the military addressed when they could. She wasn't going to leave her family without protection any longer than necessary. Plus, finding Alan and the others had been a small victory, one she wouldn't soon forget.

On the second morning, Becky was finally convinced the wound had healed enough for her to start moving again. She hated to think of how slow the trek would be with everyone on foot, but any movement was better than sitting around stagnant. She didn't feel nearly as tender as she had before and was confident the infection was nearly gone. Still, by the end of their first day hiking back to the homestead, Sarah was sore and exhausted once again. They were making good time considering half of their troop of six was kids under thirteen.

Day by day, time passed as she healed more and taught the group what she knew about survival in the wilderness. If they ever decided to leave the homestead and set off on their own, she wanted them to have the skills to be able to do so. Sarah adored Marshall, who had recently turned twelve and was the only boy right along with Cameron, who was ten, and little Pepper, who was barely three.

As they made camp on the beach at the same pier she'd slept on weeks before, Sarah watched the older children play with their little sister. She smiled and shook her head when Pepper squealed with delight at her older sibling's antics. Becky sat down next to her and beamed with pride as she watched the trio playing together.

"The kids are great, Becky. They're just so happy and chipper."

Becky chuckled. "So, are there any kids in your future?"

Sarah laughed. "Well, there are a couple of ten-year-olds back at the homestead who are kind of like my own."

"Oh really? Sounds like you and Adam really moved fast."

"Alan tell you about Adam?"

"Yeah, he told me he went up north with you, but he didn't have to. You forget how much you always talked about him and his innocence. While you claim you'd treat them all the same if you thought they were innocent, you gave Adam a lot of your attention."

"Maybe so, but we haven't had the time to even think about dating."

Becky smiled. "That's a pretty lame excuse, Sarah. I mean, it's obvious to all of us how you feel about the man. God knows he hasn't had any relations in ten years."

With everything going on around her, she hadn't even thought about Adam in days. She knew there was something special growing between them, but they didn't have the time to concern themselves with the pleasures of the world when the world was going to hell. Still, Sarah knew Becky could see right through her thoughts.

"Maybe when things start to slow down, we can work on some kind of relationship, but there's just been so much to take care of to ensure our safety that we haven't had the time to do anything else."

"There's no excuse when the man hasn't felt the touch of a woman for that long. Things might not feel like they're ideal right now, but you have all the time in the world now." Becky smiled. "Besides, any man willing to follow you to Maine on a whim has to be worth his weight in gold."

Sarah blushed as Pepper started to cry and pulled Becky away from the conversation. She'd thought she had gotten away from the interrogation, but Meredith was quick to take her friend's spot. One playful look from Meredith and Sarah groaned, knowing the conversation wasn't yet over. While there was nothing that she and Adam had done wrong, it still felt strange to be discussing the potential of a love life with a man Meredith had once strip-searched per the intake protocol.

"Come on now, you don't really think I'm that blind, now, do you?" Meredith asked.

"What are you talking about?" Sarah asked.

"You and Adam. I saw the way you two looked at each other. From the first time you laid eyes on that man, you were smitten with him."

"I was worried about an innocent man behind bars," Sarah muttered.

"I'm not arguing with that. I know you've saved many lives the same as his before, but there was always something between the two of you."

Sarah didn't know what to say to Meredith, but thankfully, she didn't have to come up with an answer. As the kids settled down for the night, Alan joined them at the small fire she'd started on the pier in an old grill someone had left behind since the last time she had been there. In earnest, she was surprised no one had taken up a more permanent shelter there. It was a good thing. Maine could become dangerous in the winter months.

She hated to think about how many people in the country weren't prepared for the cold snap ahead of them. The government wasn't going to be re-established and able to help for months. Shaking the depressing thought from her mind, Sarah smiled at her travel companions and tried to pull herself back to the conversation at hand. Alan looked like he had something on his mind but wasn't sure how to approach the topic. She sighed and focused her attention on him until he started to fidget. He quickly broke as he started to curse.

"So, if we head to Maine with you, are you sure your parents are going to be okay taking on a group like this? We don't want to intrude," Alan said.

"I'm going to be honest with you, Alan. They'd be pretty upset with me if I didn't bring you along with me."

Alan smiled. "I hope you're right. Is there going to be enough room for us to stay there long-term?"

"We made some extra room after checking the properties next to us. We have the supplies and plenty of space for you and your family. Hell, we could fit up to about ten people if we needed to. Plus, I kind of had you guys in mind when I planned it out."

"That's just like you to always think ahead. How'd they manage to be so prepared for all of this when no one else seemed to be."

"Just smart living while I was growing up. They weren't fanatics by any means, but they certainly wanted to be prepared if anything did happen. I learned a lot from them through the years."

"I'm glad you're prepared and that they were okay when you got there. How's the homestead?"

Sarah smiled. "It's nice. I didn't realize how much I missed it until I was there for a few weeks."

"Good. I know how things are down here, and I imagine it's like that everywhere. Has there been any trouble up there in that area?"

"Unfortunately, there were a couple of issues my dad had before I got there," Sarah said. "There's one local prick who's been a pain in my side, but before I left, we had put him in his place. I just don't know if it will last. He's got a dark side."

As Sarah continued to tell Alan about the villagers and the mayor, Becky and Meredith listened while the children slept. She was happy they were hearing it as well. Sooner or later, she wanted them to know what they would be up against. While the homestead was by and far a safe haven, it wasn't without its dangers, and she wanted them to be well aware of that. Sarah couldn't think of a better place for the group, but information was key to them making a decision about where to settle down.

Her heart raced as she told them about the confrontation with the mayor and his men. She hated not knowing what was happening at her parents' place. It was so strange to think about how much they had relied on technology to stay in touch before. After being away from her family for nearly ten days, Sarah was ready to be back at the farm. The homestead and the people there were everything to her, but she was still thankful she had made the journey. Not only did she have people she cared about now safe, but she also had information about the state of the rest of the world.

Home was calling her, and Sarah was ready for her travels to come to an end.

42

By the time the homestead came into view, Sarah and George were both antsy to get back to their friends and family waiting for them. As soon as he saw the twins emerge from the front gates, George started to nicker without ceasing until, finally, she let go of his bridle and let him gallop the last fifty yards to the gates. Instantly, the children were climbing on him and wrapping their arms around the horse's neck. After the warm welcome they'd given the horse, she was sure they wouldn't ever let him go again. Seconds later, as George was trotting to where his family was calling to him from the barn, the twins were climbing all over her in the same manner.

She couldn't believe how much she had missed them both. Her parents emerged a few minutes after seeing George run past the backyard. Immediately, her parents pulled her into their arms, but it was short-lived as introductions were made. Alan and Adam greeted each other like old friends. Right away, the children disappeared with the twins, leaving only Pepper behind with the adults despite the small girl's protests. Connie, as Sarah had expected, was instantly smitten with the small child and was fast to distract the child and ease the tantrum.

Sarah could see the relief in Becky's eyes as they made their way onto the property. While Adam and Connie took charge of getting the new group settled, Henry walked with Sarah to the barn to get George unpacked and back out to pasture with the other animals. From the looks of things, nothing much had changed on the homestead. The orchard was a bit more bare, and the color had gone from the grass, but as they finished harvesting, she'd expected as much. There was a huge weight lifted from her shoulders now that she had returned home.

"So, have there been any issues with the mayor while I was gone?" Sarah asked.

"Nothing with the mayor directly, but there was a problem a couple of days ago."

"Shit," Sarah said. "What happened?"

"Eric went out hunting two days ago and ran into that scout that you crossed before you left."

As soon as her father mentioned Eric's name, her blood started to boil. Anyone who was going to mess with either of those children was going to get the full amount of her rage. While she hadn't heard the full story, her heart was already racing.

"Tell me what happened, Dad."

"Well, Eric took his bow and was out in the woods hunting for rabbit. He told us that the guy came up to him and cornered him, asking a ton of questions."

"They're still trying to find out what we have here," Sarah fumed. "What was he trying to find out?"

"The main thing he was asking Eric was to find out how many people were here, but he was trying to get him to say how many guns there were and figure out what kind of resources we had."

"That son of a bitch. Is Eric okay?"

"He's fine. That's what really matters," Henry said. "He was freaked out at first, but he said the man didn't hurt him, just asked a ton of questions."

"I'm going to kill him," Sarah seethed. "If he comes back around here and shows his face, I'm going to put him down like the dying dog he is."

"Just take a breath, sweetheart. All that matters is that Eric is just fine. We don't want to start anything with them, and we certainly don't want to choose violence if we don't have to. If something happens down the road, we can deal with it then."

Sarah was still infuriated, and that wouldn't change until someone paid for scaring her little boy. Anger coursed through her as she brushed George down. Now that he was free from his gear, he was anxious to get out into the pasture with his friends. She quickly opened the gate and set him free. As she closed it again and watched him gallop to meet his friends, Sarah worked to calm herself back down. Now that she was there, she could keep them all safe. The first thing was going to be teaching them the same bird calls the girls had used.

The next time Eric was cornered, he could call out, and they'd have the man trapped. Sarah wouldn't let any of the children out of their sight again until the feud with the mayor and his men was dealt with. She wouldn't let her family live in fear. With Alan's family of five situated in the large, converted RV and Meredith in the smaller one, the children were soon racing across the property as they explored. The serious conversation the adults needed to have could wait a little longer but not forever.

There would need to be some changes to how things ran on the homestead. Sarah was sure that the scout going after Eric would precede an attack by the mayor. He was threatened by her. It came as no shock that he would wait until she was gone to attack the elderly and children, with only Adam there to defend the property. Her hatred for the man grew each time she thought about him. Before she could go down that path in her mind, an arm linked through hers, and Becky smiled at her.

"Well, you weren't wrong about this place," Becky said. "It truly is an amazing piece of land, and you guys have everything you need right here."

"It's been in the family for a while. My parents have taken care of this land and everything on it for as long as I can remember," Sarah said. "We do have a problem, but we will talk about that later."

"Is it something we need to be worried about?"

"Nothing immediate, but something we need to be watchful about, especially with the kids. We need to keep an eye out for them."

"Someone is a danger to the kids?" Becky asked.

"Not directly, but we can talk about the details later. Just promise you'll keep an eye out for anything out of place."

"That's easy. I don't think I've let them out of my sight since this whole thing started. I don't know who to trust, and I'd rather not learn the hard way."

"Good," Sarah said. "The world's gone to shit, and there was an issue the other day. I don't know what will come of it."

"Well, as long as we're here now, we're going to fight by your side. If anything were to happen to my children, I'd put someone in the grave."

"People might come to try to take what we have here, but I don't plan on letting that happen."

"You have us, and we're willing to fight to protect what's ours," Becky said.

"That's good to know. Like I said, I don't know what to expect, but a fight is what it might come down to," Sarah said. "I just don't know when or how many we'll have to fight."

As her friend went silent next to her, Sarah prayed she was worrying her for no good reason. Her biggest hope was that she was completely wrong about everything and that the scout had been a rouge working on his own. She wanted to believe they were safe, but until she dealt with the mayor herself, Sarah knew she wouldn't get a restful night's sleep. They were well armed, though, and they had so much to fight for that they wouldn't fail. It simply wasn't an option.

"Hey, have a little faith," Becky said. "I know you are worried about all this, but we are a team now. You aren't going up against this by yourself."

"I know. I just wish it wasn't an issue at all," Sarah said. "What kind of world do we live in where this is even a problem?"

"I don't think anyone ever plans on going up against an angry mob of villagers, but we'll do what we have to in order to protect our home and family now. Trust me when I tell you that it can be a lot worse. Between Alan and me, we have seven guns and two-hundred rounds of ammunition. We didn't have the bodies to defend our land because there were only two of us. Think of what we can do with seven adults."

"I know, and we aren't slouches, either. Meredith is a sharpshooter, and both my parents have damn good aim. We can make this work."

Becky nudged her affectionately. "I know we can, but it's good to see your spirit has improved a little. We are a family now; remember that."

She smiled at Becky. "We always have been. Thank you for reminding me of that."

43

*L*ater that night, as they all gathered around a large fire burning just off the porch, Sarah couldn't believe how peaceful everything felt. She never wanted the moment to change as she listened to the children playing outside. They had become fast friends, though she wasn't surprised by that. It amazed her how wonderfully the twins had flourished beneath her mother's loving care. Jamie's feisty and outspoken personality was a perfect match for Marshall's. Despite his being two years older than her, Jamie showed no fear in the face of the oldest child's bullying.

He quickly discovered that Jamie wasn't nearly as kind-hearted and docile as his younger sister. Whereas Eric and Cameron had become fast friends. As much as she was enjoying the tranquility that being back on the property had to offer, Sarah still knew the adults had a very serious conversation. They needed it to start. Every minute they didn't have sentries posted at the front of the road, Sarah grew more nervous. The mayor was obviously getting ready to take action against the homestead. She wasn't going to make anything easy on the man.

If it came down to it, Sarah wouldn't hesitate to take a life if it meant protecting her family and the people on the property. The last thing she wanted to do was let the mayor know they had more firepower and people there to defend the land. He was at expecting an easy fight, and she was going to let him keep believing that's what he would find at the homestead. Carefully keeping watch over everything while still staying hidden was going to be the adult's new primary concern. With the children distracted and happy, Sarah saw her opportunity to address the other adults on the back porch.

"Were you guys able to take an inventory of our arsenal?" Sarah asked.

"Yeah. Alan and I did a walk-through and made sure of everything we have. Looks like we have two dozen guns and fifty-five boxes of ammunition," Henry said.

She was impressed with the number of guns they had, but soon they would have to find more. There was no way of knowing how long they would have to fend for themselves, let alone how many times they would have to defend themselves. It might have sounded like a lot of ammunition to some, but with the dark days that could lay ahead of them, she wanted to be prepared.

"That's not too bad. I don't know if it will last, but I think it will get us by if the mayor tries anything."

"If not, then we could always set some traps for any others that may come," Alan said.

"If it comes to that, we'll do it. For now, I just want to have an idea of what we have and how many rounds we'll have. From the sounds of it, we'll have plenty of ammunition for the time being."

"Well, if that's not enough, there is another option. I'm just not sure if we're going to want to use it," Henry said.

"What is it that we wouldn't want to use?"

"We also have two hand grenades."

"Why in the hell do we have grenades, and where did they come from?" Sarah asked.

Alan laughed. "I was hoping to get that reaction from you. When I grabbed some weapons from the weapons stash at the prison, I grabbed a couple of grenades. I didn't know what I was going to run into, and I wanted to be prepared, just like you were always talking about."

"That makes a little more sense." Sarah chuckled.

Sarah was shocked by the surprising arsenal they had accumulated. While she couldn't see a scenario where they would need to use their grenades, they were still good to have. For the time being, she was happy with their weapons stockpile. Over time they would have to replenish their sources. It wasn't going to be easy, given how scarce ammunition had now become. Still, they had an abundance of things they could barter for in trade.

Someone in the group had to be skilled or know the basics of making bullets to boot. At one point, her father had made his own shotgun shells, and she made a mental note to ask him about it later on.

At least they were protected for the time being. The weapons were no good without shooters to fire them. They would need to start working and watching the property in shifts if they were going to catch the mayor before he attacked them. She didn't want him getting anywhere near the house. Now that they had five children living with them, keeping them safe was their main concern. Becky was a huge asset to the group as well. Her skills as a registered nurse would help them not only on the battlefield but in bartering with locals as well. If they had the ability to save even one life because she was now there, Sarah would see it as a win.

While the children were still distracted outside, Sarah wanted to make sure everyone understood their dire situation. There was no reason to worry the kids, but things were going to have to change until the confrontation with the mayor had been settled. The group had started to talk amongst themselves, but Sarah was quick to pull their attention back to the conversation at hand.

"We need to keep someone posted at all times. Until we know exactly what we're going to be dealing with, I don't want to take any chances," Sarah said. "We obviously don't want to be just sitting here on the porch, either."

"How do you want us posted?" Henry asked.

"Well, I think the best places to keep guard will be on either side of the property. I'd say if we keep to the woods, they won't have an easy line of sight on anyone."

"So, we'll stick to the wooded areas and keep watch over the property. I'll take one of the first shifts. That way, the rest of you can get some sleep," Adam said.

"That's good. I'll take the other side of the property. I'd like to be able to—"

"Sarah, as much as I know you want to keep an eye on things and be the hero we all know you are, you need to rest as much as you can," Henry said. "Adam and I can take the first watch while the rest of you sleep."

"Thank you, Dad. I just want to make sure we're all safe. Which reminds me—we need to keep an eye on the kids at all times. Don't let them get out of your sight, even for a moment."

While she wasn't sure the men would do anything to the children, she wasn't going to chance it. Any man willing to approach a child who is all alone and corner them was probably willing to do things Sarah would kill over. No, it was better to be safe and make sure the kids were all looked out for.

Now that everyone had their jobs for the night, Sarah started to feel the weight of the journey. She yawned as she stood and stretched out, the conversations dying around her as every head turned to watch. She made short work of bidding her farewells to everyone before slipping away from the group and up to her bedroom.

Before she made it all the way up the steps, Becky

pulled her to a stop and tugged at Sarah's shirt to check her wound. It was healing nicely. She hadn't mentioned the gunshot wound to either of her parents and wanted to keep it that way for a little while. They had enough to worry about without the knowledge that she had been shot. Plus, if Adam knew, he was going to flip out and want to go back to the prison to exact his revenge. She adored him for being so protective, but she didn't need more drama in their lives right now. After getting the all-clear from her friend, Sarah gave Becky a hug and headed for her room.

It felt amazing to be back in her own bed once again. She had wanted more time to talk with Adam, but that could wait until the clear and present danger was dealt with first. Being away from him and nearly dying after the altercation at the prison had changed her point of view on things. Sarah was done waiting around for him to make a move. There was obviously something between them, and she wanted to pursue it further. There weren't enough hours in the day to do everything Sarah wanted. As her eyes grew heavy, she finally started to doze off with pleasant thoughts of the future in her mind.

44

Sarah was blissfully lost in a dream when it came to a crashing halt several hours after she had dozed off. She woke with a start, pain shooting through her side at the still-fresh wound before she remembered she was no longer alone on the road and in danger. Her eyes quickly adjusted to the light from the moon outside, and she saw Adam standing over her. Sarah bolted upright. He had never been in her room before, and if he was there now, she knew there had to be a reason for it. Instantly, her eyes shot around in the dark to find the danger, but everything looked the same as when she had fallen asleep.

Outside, she could hear that everything was calm and quiet. Her heart fluttered, wondering if he was there for a more personal reason, but the concern in his eyes told her something else was going on. He jerked his head for

THE LAST HOMESTEAD

her to follow her out of the bedroom, and Sarah didn't hesitate to nod in agreement. Two minutes after he had woken her, Sarah was quietly moving to the main part of the house to join the rest of the group. The only light was two lanterns dimly burning in the kitchen. She could see the others gathered and whispering amongst themselves.

Sarah could feel the tension in the room as soon as she entered. Whatever was going on, they were obviously worried about it. Instantly, she went to the window and pulled back the curtain, but she didn't see any torches or angry mobs approaching the house. They wouldn't be safe until the mayor and his men were dealt with. Sarah was certain that until that time came, none of the adults in the house would be able to sleep easy.

"We have movement from the village," Adam said. "I can't tell for sure what's out that way, but there's definitely something."

"Did you happen to see the sentry?" Sarah asked.

"Not really. I moved up through the edge of the woods and toward the town. Once I was able to get a good line of sight on the village, I could see them starting to gather at the main entrance."

"If you had to take a guess, how many do you think were there?"

"I couldn't quite make out a solid number, but I'd easily put it around two dozen. None of them were on horseback, so they'll be coming here on foot."

Sarah knew the time had come to protect what was

rightfully theirs. She thought they would have a little more time, but looking at the family surrounding her, the fear was real. She would do whatever it took to protect them. Though she wished she could have more time to prepare for an attack, she knew the group was well-trained and ready to fight by her side.

"How long do you think we have before they get here?" Sarah asked. "Is there enough time for us to get set up?"

"I couldn't give you a good time, but from what I could tell, they were all checking their weapons and passing around ammo," Adam said.

"What are we talking about then?"

"I'd say that between the time it will take them to get ready and the time they'll take traveling here at a regular pace, we have about half an hour—tops."

Given the girth of the mayor, Sarah doubted they would be moving at anything faster than a leisurely pace. Adam hadn't mentioned seeing any animals with them, but it was still possible that the mayor had pilfered a horse from a local farm to move things along quicker. In either case, there was no time for them to wait around. They needed to have a plan in place, and she wasn't going to have their homestead shot up in the process of protecting it. As a matter of fact, she didn't want the gun-slinging drunken idiots anywhere near the farm. The group had to have a plan put together that took the posse away from the homestead.

It was nearly impossible for her not to think about the worst-case scenario. They now had five small children living on the homestead. While there was no question in her mind that the mayor didn't value their lives, Sarah saw every human as a potential for greatness. They weren't going to shoot to kill with the men, but they weren't going to let the children be put in harm's way, either. If it came down to their lives or the homesteaders, Sarah wouldn't hesitate to shoot to kill. Yet the very thought of taking another human life made her nauseous, not for herself but for her parents and her friends.

She could do what was necessary, but the weight of those actions would be harder to carry for some of the others. In particular, her mother and Becky were caregivers. They believed in healing, not killing. The group needed every able-bodied person over the age of eighteen who could shoot a weapon. Her mother's hands were unsteady thanks to years of arthritis. The best place for her was going to be watching over Pepper and the other kids while the rest of the adults dealt with the encroaching gang.

"Mom, get the kids all rounded up and take them down to the cellar," Sarah said. "The best thing you can do is to keep them safe and quiet down there while we take care of the situation up here."

"What are we going to do?" Becky asked. "Do you have a plan?"

"My only plan is to fight for what's ours and to

protect our own. We're going to grab as many guns and as much ammunition as we can."

"So, we're going to defend from the house?"

"No, I think it would be better if we plan a surprise attack and take them off guard. We're severely outnumbered, but it's likely that most of them have been drinking."

"Where would you like us to set this into motion?"

"We're going to have to move fast for this to work. We need to get to the other side of the road if we really want to take them off guard. They don't know how many people we have, and they think there are a few less than our actual number."

"We're with you, Sarah. Whatever it takes to keep this a safe place," Adam said.

"Good. I'm glad we're all on the same page here. I want to keep that gang as far from the house as possible. Whatever happens, we don't need the kids to see or hear any of it."

Alan smiled. "So, the grenades might be a little too much?"

"I wouldn't want to use them, but you never know what kind of weapons they could have. We need to get moving if we want to keep the momentum in our direction."

"All right, let's get going then," Alan said.

"There's one more thing. I don't want them to catch on too quickly," Sarah said. "Let's use bird calls to signal to each other. Let's hit them with everything we have and not give them an inch."

She could feel the fear and trepidation in the air around the group, but to their credit, they all jumped into action. Her mother and Becky had disappeared outside to get the children and bring them into the house. Despite the late hour, Henry and Alan went to the bedroom to get the rest of their weapons. Sarah quietly went to the twin's bedroom and woke them both, telling them to grab their blankets and pillows. They were streetwise children who knew Sarah wasn't telling them everything from the very beginning. Yet neither argued when she insisted they were going to have a sleepover with the others in the cellar.

Sarah knew Connie was going to make the event a fun one for all five of the children, despite the terrifying chaos about to happen outside the homestead. She waited until Connie and the kids were safely in the cellar before bringing out the arsenal of weapons from her parents' bedroom. When every adult besides her mother was strapped down with two to three guns each, they split into two groups and headed out the front door. Alan, Henry, and Meredith were going to take the far side of the road, moving parallel to Becky, Sarah, and Adam on the homestead side.

The group moved out silently as her heart started to pound in her ears. In the stillness of the night, Sarah was sure they would have an advantage over the approaching people. Among her group were a few sharpshooters and seasoned marksmen. They were sober, scared, and protective of the property and people on the land. They were going to win because they had more to fight for. Losing to the men was simply not an option for the homesteaders.

45

Even as they moved, Sarah was worried about the group. They were outnumbered four to one if what Adam had seen was accurate. Sarah knew between the sharpshooters they had on their side and the advantage of a surprise attack, there was a chance they would succeed. Still, she was grateful that she had given the order not to shoot to kill. At the very least, they would save a few lives that way. Everyone had their guns loaded and ready to go so there would be no time wasted in switching the weapons over when the moment came.

Hopefully, because of their preparedness, they would give the illusion of double the numbers they really had. Sarah was hoping the men weren't coming for the homesteaders, but her gut told her they were. She would take her own instincts over others any day of the week. With that knowledge in mind, they moved roughly one hundred yards away from the edge of the homestead on the road and hunkered down to wait for the gang.

Despite feeling beyond ready for the pending confrontation, Sarah could see that her companions were on edge. Their nerves were going to affect their ability to shoot straight and hit the targets in the designated areas. She didn't want to spend her afternoon hauling bodies off the road. As soon as the men gave up, Sarah would issue a ceasefire to try to negotiate their surrender. She had to talk to the others and make sure they understood how much their nerves were going to affect the shooting about to take place. It was going to be terrifying for the children to hear, even from the safety of the cellar.

The faster they could get it over with, the better. With every shot that rang out, Sarah knew her mother would be living a nightmare. When Adam approached her, Sarah smiled at him. They still had a few minutes before the men would be passing through if they were, in fact, headed for the homestead. Not having solid proof that they were heading in that direction, though, was eating away at her.

"Is everything all right?" Adam asked. "You seem to be deep in thought or, at the very least, worried about something."

"I'm just wondering if the group is even coming this way," Sarah said. "They could just be out scavenging, and this could all be for nothing."

"Do you really think they would gather that many men just to go around and see what they can find? I mean, it's possible, but I don't think that's what they were preparing for."

"I don't know. I really don't like the idea of shooting them without giving them the option to turn around a go back. It just doesn't seem right."

Sarah knew their lives were resting on her shoulders. While they all had their own minds and could make the decisions for themselves, she had become their leader in a way. They looked to her for answers, and there were just times that would come when she didn't know if she could give them the right ones. The more she thought about the incoming mob, the more she worried about the souls that could be lost. Not just from the dead but their own if they made choices that could be taken as less than humane. Adam's voice ripped her from her thoughts.

"Well, what are you thinking, then?"

"Honestly, I just don't know yet," Sarah said. "Have everyone hold their positions for a few minutes."

"What are you going to do?" Adam asked. "We're all in this together, but I'd like to know what you're doing."

"I'm going to move up a little and see if I can get my eyes on them. I'll only be a minute, but I have to try to figure this out before we make a move we all regret."

"All right, I'll let them know to hold."

Sarah wasn't yet sure what she was going to do. All she knew was she was going to have a hard time shooting at them without some sort of confirmation that they were after her homestead. As she quietly moved through the dark forest, she listened for any sounds of others on the road. Her hope was to hear them talking about their plan before they reached the homestead. That would still give the group the element of surprise while giving her the verification she so desperately needed.

She continued to move as she put a little more distance between herself and the group waiting for her in the forest before the homestead. Unfortunately, they didn't have nearly as much time as she had hoped as the posse came into view fifty feet ahead of her on the road. They were moving with a surprising amount of speed, given the size of some of the men. Just as she had suspected, the mayor had commandeered himself a horse along with a few others for his men. She quietly cursed under her breath. The animals complicated things.

It limited the number of shots they could take without injuring the horses or killing the men. If it came down to it, Sarah would take killing the man over injuring the horses. The animals had done nothing wrong. The humans, on the other hand, were making the conscious choice to steal from the homesteaders. She wasn't going to live in fear for the rest of the time that the world was in the dark. If the mayor and his men wanted a battle, she was going to make sure they got one.

After a moment or two, the group moved closer, and she was able to hear some of the conversations taking place among the men in the mob. At first, it was hard to make out what any of them were saying. They all seemed to be talking over one another, but once the group started to spread out, she heard two men talking clearly.

Sarah tried to stay low to the ground, but she needed to learn what they were actually trying to do.

"Man, have you heard about this place?"

"No, not really. I was just told to grab a gun and come along."

"I've heard this homestead has everything. It's a gold mine for the apocalypse." The man laughed. "They got booze in there, along with food, firewood, livestock, and my personal favorite, women."

"Hell, I'd settle for some good booze and a woman right now. I hope the reports are right," the second man said. "I wouldn't mind getting both my whistles wet."

The first man nearly fell over from laughing so hard. "Before you know it, we're going to be eating and fornicating like wild animals all winter long. Talk about the best way to stay warm."

"It's our duty to take the women. They'll need us to get through the winter as much as we'll need them."

"You're right about that."

"Will the two of you shut the hell up," the mayor snapped. "We don't want to scare those bitches away. If you want half of what you're talking about, we need to take this place without an incident."

"How much farther is it?"

"We're about half a mile from the homestead, so let's keep the talking to a minimum. We have the element of surprise on our side, boys."

Her blood was boiling as she quietly snuck ahead of the group back to where hers was waiting. As she moved, she listened for any indication that her approach and departure had been noticed, but there was none from the posse. Sarah wanted to put a bullet into the two men who had been talking. It would be a cold day in hell before she let them do anything to the women on the homestead. Thinking about the young children in the cellar, Sarah forced all emotion to leave her mind. She had to keep a clear head if they were going to succeed in the mission.

She took her position a few yards away from the other two just as the sun started to peak into the sky. Unless they were being carefully looked for, no one would notice the six shooters spread out over a few dozen yards on either side of the road. It was the perfect setup, the layout everything she wanted in an ambush. All around her, the world was silent except for nature. When she heard the encroaching footsteps and voices of the men marching down the road, Sarah gave a familiar birdcall to the others across the road.

It was the signal they had been waiting for as the group readied themselves for the attack. The tension in the air was nearly palpable as the gang came into view and inched closer to their trap. No one was going to take her land.

46

Sarah didn't need to be able to see the others across the street and to her left to know they were prepared for what was about to come. After hearing the men in the group talk to each other, she was resolved in her decision to launch a preemptive attack on them. There was no longer any question in her mind that they were coming to do terrible things to her home and her family. As the first row of men passed by her, laughing and joking to themselves about what they were going to do, Sarah held her breath and steadied her aim. None of the others would fire off a shot until they heard hers ring out.

It wasn't time yet. She had to wait a few more seconds if she wanted them all to be in a clear line of fire. When she could see the end of the group, Sarah let out the breath she had been holding and took aim at one of the last of the men's legs. Squeezing the trigger, the shot rang out over the silent terrain for a split second before the second shower of bullets attacked the men. Instantly, the air was filled with gunfire and screaming. Sarah's heart was racing as she took aim at one man after another. Of the group, five were on horseback, including the mayor. She took extra caution with those individuals and managed to knock off all of them between her gunfire and her family's.

When the few individuals still standing dropped their guns in surrender, Sarah called for a ceasefire. She didn't waste any time asking the fallen gang if they were surrendering. While several of them called out, Sarah didn't hear the mayor's voice assuring her they would not shoot. Still, it was a calculated risk she was willing to take. She kept her weapon at the ready as she slowly stepped out into the clearing behind the group of downed men. Instantly, every pair of eyes in the group turned to glare at her. Sarah didn't care. They were all still moving and didn't appear to have any immediate casualties. She was proud of the work her family had done.

She looked around, and after several moments, Sarah found the mayor off to the side of the rest of the men who were giving up. As she approached the man who called himself the town's leader, she noticed he was bleeding from his arm. She could tell quickly that it was only a minor wound and the man would be fine with some time to heal.

"Your men are giving up, and you've taken a bullet as

it is," Sarah said. "Next time, we won't be shooting to wound. We'll be taking the shots that make it so you don't get to have a life, understand?"

The man nodded.

"Now, for all of you who can hear me now. Your reign of terror is going to end now. You are welcome to stay in the village, but it's going to come with certain rules. If I hear anything about any more brutality, I'll personally execute any of the people who are responsible."

"You're going to let us go?" one man asked.

"Yes, but if I find out that you haven't changed your ways, I'm going to come looking for you, and the results will be different. Does everyone understand?"

There were several who agreed with her and a few others who nodded. Sarah never wanted to hurt anyone, but they had ideas of their own that she couldn't stand by and allow to happen. As she glanced around at the men who followed the mayor, it looked like they were all afraid for their lives. She knew the fear they felt alone would lead them in a different direction in life.

"Now, I need to make sure you all understand the consequences you'll face if you defy my orders. Does anyone have a problem with anything I've said?"

Looking around their group, Sarah noticed right away that none of the men would meet her gaze this time. They were obviously beaten and terrified about what was going to come next. Several of them were already trying to stand and get away from her and the invisible army she had in the forest. They weren't having much success. They would need to work together to get their wounded back to the village in time to save everyone. Still, Sarah had no pity for the group. It wasn't her fault they were sheep following a maniacal mayor. They had made their decision, knowing how much damage their actions would cause to Sarah and her family.

She loved that they had no way of knowing how many of them there were. It was a detail she would keep to herself. Sarah wasn't going to let the men leave so easily. Not with all the ammunition the group had wasted while going after the posse. Sarah wanted some retribution for the men's actions. The lives they could potentially lose and the pain they were enduring were not enough. What would stop them from going back, handing off their guns to someone else, and letting another round of villagers finish what they had started?

"Not so fast," Sarah yelled. "No one is leaving until they drop all of their weapons!"

The men who were already starting to flee turned back, and for a moment, she could see them considering running despite her orders. She lifted her gun a mere few inches, and the fleeing men quickly dropped their weapons before continuing to run. Sarah couldn't help but smile as the others followed in the same suit. Her eyes narrowed on the mayor. She hadn't yet decided if he would be able to flee as easily as his minions. She vaguely remembered a saying about cutting the head off a snake, and at that moment, it sounded like a wonderful idea.

"What about you, Mr. Mayor?" she hissed.

"Yeah, I have a damn problem with it," the mayor said as he stood up.

"Well, I'd look around if I were you. It seems to me you're the only person here who has an issue with what I'm saying," Sarah said. "Let's ask them, shall we? Does anyone have a problem here?"

Again, none of his men met her gaze. She knew he was alone in his stand, and so did he. Without men to back him up, Sarah hoped he would back down and return to what little life he could have. Judging by the way he glared at her, it wasn't going to be as easy as she had hoped.

"There's nothing left here for you to fight with, Mayor. It's over, and you've lost. Just let it go. We can all live in harmony together, or you can go out by yourself and try to make it on your own. The choice is yours."

"If you think this is over, you've got another think coming," he seethed. "This isn't over by a long shot. I'll hunt you down, and then I'll hunt down every person you have here with you. I'll find others who will follow me. Bigger and stronger men than these."

Sarah scoffed and turned before turning back to the delusional man. "You're a rabid dog, and you need to be put down. If you want to play that game, we can play, but you won't like the outcome. Then again, you won't be around to like or dislike anything. Walk away while I'm still giving you a choice in the matter."

"You're going to regret this. I promise you that."

"Walk away. It's the last time I'm telling you." Sarah glared at the man.

Sarah turned away from the mayor and started to walk in the direction of the guns that the fleeing posse had left on the ground. She was happy the entire event had transpired without any lives lost. Plus, they had recovered more than what they needed in weapons and ammunition. Sarah wasn't a heartless person. She knew some of the men were simply led astray or threatened by the mayor into joining up with him. Several of the guns were shotguns that were the only source people had for hunting now.

Honestly, she knew in the days and weeks to come, if any one of the men approached her and asked for the guns back in a respectful and apologetic manner, Sarah would gladly return them and hopefully make a new friend. All she wanted was to live a peaceful existence for herself and her family but also for the villagers as well. No one deserved to live under a tyrannical leader like the mayor. Suddenly, she heard something behind her and quickly spun around just in time to see the large man lunging at her with a blade in his hand.

47

Despite spinning around, there were only a few feet between her and the mayor. He had a small knife in his hand, and his eyes were full of rage. Just as the man moved, she tried to lunge away from him, but the stitches in her side ripped, and she screamed out. Mere seconds had passed, but it felt like an eternity as he swung the weapon at her. She didn't have time to react. A single shot rang out through the quiet morning. Sarah had half expected to feel the sting of a bullet again when suddenly the mayor lurched forward and toppled onto her.

Sarah felt like she was suffocating beneath the enormous weight of the man. She felt something warm on her shoulder and prayed she hadn't been shot. There was no pain besides the man on top of her. Instantly, though, she was aware of the fact that her side was aching to the point that it felt like she had been shot again. She wanted to cry but didn't want the others to see as they ran forward and dragged the man's body off her. Adam was at her side in an instant, pulling her to her feet gently as he looked her over. She was touched by the concern she saw in his eyes. Every step she took, though, she winced with pain. Sarah was unable to stop herself.

Perhaps she had pushed her body too far for the last time, and it was finally giving up on her. As Adam helped her to the edge of the road, she held on to him. Her mind was still spinning from the encounter and undoubtedly from smacking against the hard pavement of the road when the mayor had fallen onto her.

"Sarah, are you all right?" Adam asked. "You look like you took a pretty hard fall when he landed on you. I want you to tell me if everything is okay."

"Honestly, I think I'm just worn the hell out. It's been a long few weeks, and I'm just tired. Other than that, I'm good. I promise."

Without hesitating, Adam pulled her into his arms. The weight of his body against hers made her feel like she was more safe than she had ever felt before. The warmth of his touch had a secure feel to it, and the longer he held her, the more comfortable she felt. For a moment, she didn't want to move from where they were. After all the time she had wondered what his arms would feel like when they wrapped around her, the time was finally there.

"I was so worried about you," Adam whispered. "I was

scared I was going to lose you before I really ever had you. I don't ever want to lose you, Sarah."

"I'm okay, Adam. I'm not going anywhere."

Sarah was blown away by his revelation. Though she had known for a long time that he had feelings for her and that her feelings for him were the same, they never had actually talked about it. From the moment the world was thrown into darkness, they were forced to face one challenge after another, but never the challenge right in front of them.

"I know you're fine now, but I thought I was going to lose you through this entire situation. It made me realize how I really feel about you, and I don't want to go another minute without you in my life."

Sarah smiled. "Yeah? So, tell me how you really feel about me."

"I care about you more than I ever realized when I thought I'd never see you again. I don't want to feel that way ever again. I love you, Sarah. I think I have for a very long time."

"Oh, Adam. I'm glad you've finally told me. I didn't know how to say it myself, but I feel the same way about you."

Sarah didn't want to talk anymore as she pulled Adam's face down and kissed his lips passionately. The fireworks ignited inside of her as he wrapped his arms around her and held her close. All around them, their friends and family started to cheer as they worked on picking up the weapons left behind. She didn't care, not pulling away from him until she knew it was going to go beyond what was publicly acceptable. There would be plenty of time for romance now that the only threat to the homestead had been neutralized.

As they went back to help the others gather the weapons, Sarah instructed the men to bury the mayor's body on the other side of the road while the women got the weapons inside and secured them in her parents' bedroom. They could do a complete inventory later. She knew her mother was going to be anxious to know what was going on, and the children had to be terrified. As the sun peeked over the trees and they started walking back to the house, Sarah saw her mother peeking out the curtain and waved.

A few seconds later, the children came racing through the front door into her arms and those of their mother. They had taken the time to unload all of the guns before gathering them up into two large bags. Now, with the children in their arms and grateful that no one was injured, they were able to set them down, where Alan and Adam quickly scooped them up and took them inside. When her mother came out and joined them, Sarah couldn't help but embrace the woman. It had been her strength that had gotten the children through the ordeal. She was the rock and the foundation of the family.

"So, can we safely say this is all over now?" Connie asked. "Do we need to worry about them coming back?"

"Well, the mayor is dead, and the others are gone,"

Sarah replied. "We made them give up their weapons before we let them leave, so I don't think they'll come back. I don't think we're going to have more problems from them."

Connie let out a sigh and smiled. She was glad to see her mother's shoulders finally relax since she knew the thought of all the gunshots ringing out must have had her dreading the outcome. As she smiled at her mother, Adam made his way to her side and pulled Sarah close to him. Kissing her cheek, he happily smiled down at her. She could get lost in his arms for the rest of time.

"Well, I'm glad to see you finally look happy. It seems to me that everything is just about perfect now."

"It's starting to feel that way, that's for sure," Sarah said. "I'm just glad it's over, and we can move on with our lives without being targeted."

Connie chuckled. "Well, it took the world coming to an end for mine and your father's wish for you to come true."

"What wish would that be?"

"To find love, of course. We always knew you would, but I can't believe it took an actual act of God for it to happen."

Sarah laughed. "I think it took two acts of God. Between them finally proving Adam was innocent and the end of the world, I finally found the love of my life. I definitely didn't think it would happen."

"All I can say is that it's about damn time," Henry said. "End of the world or not, I'm happy for you, sweetheart."

Sarah couldn't believe everything was finally over. The only black spot on their otherwise perfectly gathered family was knowing that John was still at the prison fighting against the inmates who had overtaken it. She hated that he wasn't there, and he was constantly in her prayers, but there was nothing she could do about it until this spring when they had the forces and nature on their side. Only then could they make a pilgrimage to help get him out.

Until then, she was going to relish what happiness they had found. Not only had she found someone who shared her views and seemed to adore her family as much as she did, but they were also all safe and would stay that way throughout the ordeal. Sarah knew she would finally be able to sleep easy at night, though they still had a long way to go. While they would keep up having a sentry watching over the homestead in the evenings, the mayor was no longer a threat. She had made the message clear. Harmony Homestead was not to be trifled with.

They were not going to back down from a fight, but they were not going to turn their backs on their fellow man, either. When the villagers needed them, they would come to their aid. Hopefully, word would spread that the homestead was a safe haven but a well-protected one as well.

EPILOGUE

As Sarah curled up onto the couch next to Adam and took a sip of her hot cocoa, she watched the children and Becky lighting the delicate candles on top of the tree. They had spent weeks making the decorations that now adorned the house and the property. Everything was truly picturesque. Snow had started to fall days before, and without a weather forecast, she had no idea how long it would continue. It was unlike anything she had ever seen before, though, and she knew the other adults felt the same. The pristine, white landscape was untouched by machines and men for the most part.

They spent their afternoons tracking small winter game and keeping the houses warm while bonding and teaching the children everything the collective had knowledge about. Over the months since the villagers and the mayor had attacked them, at least fifty had since set up trading routes with the homesteaders. Sarah knew the homestead was a popular place for people to now come not only for trading and supplies but for medical insight as well. Becky had been a huge asset to their group, right along with the rest of them. Each one offered a different well of knowledge.

As the children started to open the homemade gifts that everyone had put together, there was a knock at the door. Despite everything being calm, Sarah immediately tensed as she set down her mug and glanced at Adam. He reached for his weapon as she moved toward the door. Peeking out through the glass, Sarah gasped and quickly jerked it open. The man looked more like an abominable snowman than a human, but she would have recognized his eyes anywhere as she quickly pulled him into the warmth of the house. To her complete and utter disbelief, it was John. Their long-lost friend had finally made it to them.

"What in the hell happened to you, John?" Sarah asked. "How'd you get here?"

"Well, it's been a pain, but I helped some of the locals take back the prison," John replied. "After they had it well fortified and protected, I left in search of the homestead you spoke so much about."

"I'm glad you made it."

"So am I. To be fair, you left an easy trail to follow if a person knew what to look for. You certainly made an impact along the way."

"Well, you know me. I can't believe you're finally here. I've been hoping to make my way down there in the spring."

"Now there's no need to." John smiled. "That reminds me, I brought you a present."

John reached into his pack and pulled out a portable HAM radio. Turning it on, he handed it over to Sarah.

"Merry Christmas. The message should start again at any time. It started this morning, and it's the first radio address to come out since this whole thing started."

Moments later, the radio came to life, and they all quietly listened to what the president was saying.

"Merry Christmas to all the people across the United States. It may come as a surprise to many of you that we finally have some radio frequencies up and working. Well, I'm here to tell you that this is just the start of many good things to come. While we are a nation that is going to take time to heal and repair ourselves, the new year will bring plenty more good news.

We will bring power back to this country, and we will rebuild. I promise there is still a bright future for everyone. I'll follow this up with any updates I can until the day we are back to where we were before the solar storm. This isn't a country that surrenders to anything. We will grow stronger, and we will persevere through these hard times. Again, Merry Christmas. Through the next year, power will be restored to many of you. Hold on and stand proud. We're survivors."

Her heart felt like it was going to burst with joy as Adam held her close, and the tears started to fall. They had to spread the good news to the villagers and everyone else as well. The nation was healing. They were going to be whole again. Finally, Sarah had gotten her happily ever after. Even if it took the world coming to an end for it to happen.

Made in the USA
Monee, IL
05 December 2023